"CODY, A

Rachel whi

moving natu

When the light went out moments later, Razor knew his senses were being tested. Faulty wiring or coincidence he'd accept, but ghostly invervention he refused to acknowledge.

Still, he couldn't dismiss the feel of Rachel trembling in his arms. Nor could he stop himself from lowering his head, from feeling some kind of magnetic pull that drew his lips to hers. Anticipation burned hot as he found her mouth and felt it open beneath his touch.

Warm, dangerous feelings swirled around them, mixed with the scents of their bodies and intensified into a force field of sensation. He couldn't see and neither could she. Here, pressed together, they were equal and they were on fire. . . .

WHAT ARE *LOVESWEPT* ROMANCES?

They are stories of true romance and touching emotion. We believe those two very important ingredients are constants in our highly sensual and very believable stories in the LOVESWEPT *line. Our goal is to give you, the reader, stories of consistently high quality that may sometimes make you laugh, sometimes make you cry, but are always fresh and creative and contain many delightful surprises within their pages.*

Most romance fans read an enormous number of books. Those they truly love, they keep. Others may be traded with friends and soon forgotten. We hope that each LOVESWEPT *romance will be a treasure—a "keeper." We will always try to publish*

LOVE STORIES YOU'LL NEVER FORGET
BY AUTHORS YOU'LL ALWAYS REMEMBER

The Editors

Loveswept® 636

THE MORNING AFTER

SANDRA CHASTAIN

BANTAM BOOKS

NEW YORK · TORONTO · LONDON · SYDNEY · AUCKLAND

THE MORNING AFTER

A Bantam Book / September 1993

ISBN 0-553-44272-4

Published simultaneously in the United States and Canada

Bantam Books are published by Bantam Books, a division of Bantam Doubleday Dell Publishing Group, Inc. Its trademark, consisting of the words "Bantam Books" and the portrayal of a rooster, is Registered in U.S. Patent and Trademark Office and in other countries. Marca Registrada. Bantam Books, 1540 Broadway, New York, New York 10036.

PRINTED IN THE UNITED STATES OF AMERICA

OPM 0 9 8 7 6 5 4 3 2 1

AUTHOR'S NOTE

Special thanks to Donna Ball, who, without knowing why, read the tarot cards for Razor Cody, and, later, Razor and Rachel Kimble. All the cards fell just as described and represent the actual interpretation rendered. Any misrepresentation of the procedure is mine and not that of Donna Ball.

Also, thanks to Ellen Tabor, who shared with me her magical memories of Savannah and its ghosts, and to Kathryn Falk, who selected such a romantic spot as the site of her Tenth Annual Booklovers Conference.

ONE

The woman stood in the doorway, a silhouette etched in gold. The light shining from behind her illuminated an ethereal creature who might have come straight out of a child's fairy tale.

He hadn't rung the bell. In fact Razor Cody hadn't been at all certain that he'd found the right house. Instead of the proud, restored Victorian mansion he'd been expecting, the narrow, decrepit house was sandwiched between two others, hanging back a step as if it were ashamed of its shabby exterior.

But what held his attention wasn't the house, it was the woman. She was a fantasy, a princess, with hair the color of spun gold framing a mysterious face hidden by the shadows.

He hadn't expected this. He hadn't expected the

tightness in his chest that made it hard to breathe either.

"Are you Miss Rachel Kimble?"

"You've come," she said in a low, breathless voice, giving credence to the fantasy. "I've been expecting you."

"How is that?"

"When Harry left, he said you'd come."

"Harry?" He'd found her. At last he'd found the right woman. "I don't doubt that," Razor said sharply. "Knowing Harry, I don't doubt that at all."

She didn't answer, but the tilt of her chin suggested a calm acceptance of the tension that suddenly hung in the air between them.

"Where is he?" Razor finally asked, remaining as still as the woman.

Through the open door, he caught the scent of a subtly illusive perfume that, under other circumstances, might have intrigued the senses of a man who'd been described as too hard to notice such things. The aroma suggested the Orient perhaps, or maybe some long-forgotten fragrance from the South Seas.

"Where is who?"

"Harry, that low-down crook. I warn you, lady, I want him. If he isn't here, I'll wait. I intend to have my revenge."

"Why would you want to harm Harry?"

"Because I let that smooth-talking confidence man convince me to take him on as a partner. As a result I lost my construction company, my reputation, and most of my assets."

"Oh dear," Rachel murmured. "What did Harry do to cause that?"

"He used inferior products and took shortcuts on construction. Then, when the hotel we were building collapsed, Harry disappeared, leaving me to take the blame."

Rachel Kimble had known this man was coming. Now, as he stood on her porch in the darkness, her vision of his face was as clear as it had been the first time she'd seen him and, for the weeks since, when he'd become a special part of her dreams. She hadn't known his name, nor when he'd arrive—only that he would come.

A bead of perspiration rolled down between her breasts, and she realized that her whole body was responding to his presence. She'd known what would happen, too, but she hadn't understood how strong the feelings would be.

He was tall, powerful, even dangerous. She could feel the rigidly held emotion strumming through him, like distant music in the night. Yes, she thought, dark, both inside and out, with wicked, strong eyes that cut through her, firing the heat that curled and flickered in the pit of her stomach.

4

"Of course you'll wait," she whispered, moving aside to permit him to enter. "I wasn't sure how you'd find me, but I knew you would. Now I understand. Harry sent you to me."

"Sent me? Not on your life, Miss Rachel. In fact I'm reasonably certain that Harry doesn't want me here—not if he plans to hang on to that tiger-colored head of hair and those whiskers he's so proud of. When I get my hands on him, I intend to shave both, before I separate him from his head."

Rachel wasn't worried by his threat. His anger was understandable, for it came from the same powerful force that kindled the fire between them. But there was an underlying sense of urgency in the man's tightly wound voice. It vibrated in the air and feathered her cheeks with menace. She shivered. She tingled. Beneath her long skirt, her cat, Witchy, rubbed against her ankles, purring the strange sound that announced her unease.

Still Rachel waited. She couldn't have misinterpreted the vision. Even if she hadn't seen him repeatedly in her dreams, the one time she'd dared to ask, her special cards had predicted his arrival. She couldn't have made a mistake. He couldn't be the wrong man. It had never occurred to her that he wouldn't understand.

"Miss Kimble. That is your last name, isn't it?"

She nodded. He didn't understand. That would

make the situation more difficult. But she'd work it out. For now it was best that she be patient with him. "Yes, I'm Rachel Kimble. But you have me at a disadvantage. I don't know your name."

"That's right, you don't. Do you always invite perfect strangers into your home?"

"Perfect?" She gave a little laugh, throwing back her head. Yes, he *was* the one she'd expected. "Oh, my fantasy man, I don't know much about you, but I doubt that 'perfect' would apply, and if you were perfect, we wouldn't fit together."

As the light unveiled her face, Razor felt a burst of unexpected fire hit him somewhere in the area of his groin. Wearing an ankle-length print skirt and some kind of off-the-shoulder lavender blouse, she was the most beautiful woman he'd ever seen. With huge violet eyes and a head of tousled blond hair that spilled across her bare shoulders like a golden cape, she was breathtaking—nothing like he'd expected.

And she was wrong. She was perfect.

There was honesty and passion there, which seemed to complement a spiritual kind of innocence. She was staring at him, not with fear but with question in the tilt of her head, eyes wide with something akin to wonder.

But more, there was a curious kind of calmness about her. In the face of his vocal threat she simply waited, her lips parted, her breathing light and quick.

Over the years he'd known many women, enough to handle himself in almost any situation. But this woman didn't fit the mold. He couldn't put his finger on what was so different about her, but the quiet assurance of her whispery voice reached out and touched him like a physical caress.

"Miss Kimble, only my mother could find any perfection in me," he said, forcing some of the tightness from his voice. "And she was prejudiced."

"I'm glad. Mothers ought to think their children are perfect."

"And they're quite often blind."

Rachel blanched, dropping her hand from the door and stepping back. She'd never known her mother. She'd been raised in an orphanage by nuns. She'd never had a family at all—until Harry.

"Seeing what we want to see instead of the truth," she said softly, "is sometimes a gift. When we can no longer see reality, we create it, Mr. . . ."

"Cody, Razor Cody. Now, if you'll direct me to Harry, I'll not take up any more of your time."

"Oh, but you will," she said. How could she make him understand? Now that he was there, her life was changing and she couldn't stop it. She'd been moving toward this moment for two years. Suddenly she was afraid.

"No, I'll go, as soon as I find Harry."

"No, you won't. You'll take up a great deal of my time, Mr. Cody," she went on as if he hadn't spoken. "Bring your bag inside and close the door. Come, Witchy, let's make our guest some tea. Will it be blackberry or China? Or perhaps our own special blend?"

Razor hadn't expected it to be easy to find Harry. The entire Atlanta police department couldn't do that, but Razor had known about Miss Rachel, living in Savannah, Georgia. Harry's big mistake, while he was deliberately ruining Razor, was referring to Rachel, over and over. Sometimes with pride, sometimes concern. Always as "the beautiful Miss Rachel." But, without a last name, it had taken Razor some time to find her. Miss Rachel turned out to be a surprise.

He watched as she moved serenely down the hallway, past the faded wallpaper and worn carpet as if she were walking the halls of some Italian castle.

Razor had the same sensation he'd once had in a house of mirrors, as if what he was seeing wasn't real, as if the floor beneath his feet were shifting, not attached to the ground. After a moment he shook off the illusion that he had stepped back in time and he followed her.

Again he wondered what kind of woman invited a stranger in and offered him tea? She'd been waiting for him, expecting him. Surely she had confused his arrival with that of someone else. Razor was acutely uncomfortable with that thought. How could she have expected him, and if she had, what did she expect him to do?

Surely she wasn't a con artist like Harry.

No, that didn't match the slightly melancholy feel to the run-down house he was seeing. Nor did the house match the mansion Harry had bragged about providing for his Miss Rachel. It was more of a row house, the narrow corridor running alongside a small parlor and the staircase leading up. He stopped, leaning against an odd-shaped floor-to-ceiling post that formed the final pillar at the base of the stair rail.

Something was wrong.

Something was eerie.

Something was making Razor feel little twinges of cold across his face and down his backbone, almost as if he were being touched with icy fingertips.

"Damn! Where are you, Harry?"

From the end of the corridor he heard the cat meow almost as if she were answering. Everything was very strange.

"Mr. Cody?"

Razor let go of the post and moved toward the light and the sound of Rachel Kimble's voice as she talked to the cat.

The kitchen had been turned into an old-fashioned parlor, complete with a fireplace in which the coals were still glowing on an October night that wasn't even cool. At least he hadn't thought it was when he'd come in. Now he wasn't certain. The house seemed awash with air currents. Old house, he decided. Obviously the bay window could use fresh caulking.

A small table was draped with a cabbage-rose-print skirt over which a solid pink-fringed shawl had been thrown. Hanging from the ceiling over the table was a pink-fringed lamp, giving out a soft, warm glow. Razor had the feeling that he'd stepped back into the 1800s.

Rachel was taking delicate China cups from a beveled-glass-fronted cabinet and carefully placing them on saucers with lace paper doilies in the bottom. He watched her exaggeratedly slow movements as the teapot began to whistle. In the bay window the black cat lay, its gold eyes watching Razor's examination of the room.

"Would you like cream and sugar, or lemon, in your tea, Mr. Cody?"

"Doesn't matter, Miss Kimble. I'm not much into tea and crumpets."

A light laugh. "I'm afraid there are no crumpets. I've never even eaten crumpets; have you?"

"No. I'm more a coffee-and-doughnuts kind of man."

"Yes, I can believe that. There's an energy about you. Perhaps it comes from heat generated by the sugar you consume."

Heat? Hell, yes. He didn't know whether it was the fire or the light, but from the moment he stepped into the house, his body temperature had started to rise. He'd attributed it to anger, or humidity like the New Orleans climate from which he'd come. Fall in Savannah was hot and humid as well. But the heat didn't jibe with the odd flashes of cold that touched him now and then. Maybe he was coming down with something.

"No, you're not ill," she answered as if he'd voiced his thoughts.

"I sense it too," she admitted. "I'd heard about such physical awareness between people, but I think it's far too soon to act on our feelings. Still, the tickley sensation is very nice, isn't it?"

His legs seemed to buckle and he found himself sitting at the table with the shawl's fringe skimming his knees. *Physical awareness? Too soon?*

"I'm afraid that I haven't had any experience with this kind of thing," she went on. "What shall we do?"

"Whoa! I don't know what's happening here, Miss Kimble, but I don't think I understand."

Mr. Cody wasn't doing any better. That helped. Rachel wondered if she dared tell him that he would be her first lover. Women didn't become twenty-four years of age and remain a virgin in today's world. But she had. There'd been no first crush, no teenage sweetheart. There'd been little opportunity in a girls' school, and by the time she'd graduated, she'd learned to avoid relationships. Friends, yes, a few, but nothing more.

The sisters always promised that one day the woman who'd left her at the school would come back for her. She never had. And one by one, as the other children were adopted, Rachel understood. Don't get close. Caring hurts. The people she cared about always went away.

Even Harry.

She understood about people being temporary. She understood that Razor was to be special, but he didn't understand—yet. It was all up to her. "Do call me Rachel. Prefacing it with 'Miss' makes me feel very old. I think I'll give you blackberry. You sound like a dark man with deep, wild passion."

She added a measure of tea to a smaller pot and, anchoring the pot firmly with her fingers, positioned the kettle over it and filled it with the steaming liquid. She turned away, allowing the tea to steep while she brought sugar and cream to the table.

Finally she poured the lilac-colored liquid into his cup and held it out to him.

"Aren't you having any?"

"Oh, yes. I'm having my own special mix." She dropped a homemade cloth tea bag into her cup and poured in water from the teapot.

"How come you get a special blend and I get the commercial kind?"

"Because I don't know you well enough yet to create a blend for you. For now you'll like the blackberry. Why don't you try it?"

And Razor was drinking blackberry tea and liking it, when he'd never before cared for tea that wasn't strong, sweet, and poured over ice.

"Tell me why *you* think you're here, Mr. Cody."

Razor wasn't interested in chitchat. He'd never been one for casual conversation, and this was certainly no exception. Still he heard himself saying, in a voice that at least passed for pleasant, "If I'm to drop the 'Miss,' I think you can drop the 'Mister'."

"Fair enough, Cody."

He noticed that she skipped over his nickname, using his last name instead. That was another odd thing. Though men often called each other by a last name, nobody ever called Razor anything but Razor.

Rachel lifted the bag from her cup and squeezed

out the last drop of liquid, then laid it on her saucer as she took a sip of her tea. "Well?"

"Why am I here? I said before that I'm looking for Harry."

"I wish I could help you, but I haven't seen Harry since he bought this house and moved me here."

"But you have heard from him?"

"Oh, yes. I heard from him about eight months ago. He said there was a job he had to finish, something to do with a man he'd set up in business."

Razor groaned. Harry hadn't even tried to keep his plans for a life of crime a secret. "Set up? He did that all right. Set me up for jail."

"Jail? You've been in jail? How unfortunate."

"Jail was the end result. It came after I lost everything else and was left with a fine that I couldn't pay. After I turned everything I had into cash to pay my fine, I still had to spend a few months in jail."

"That seems harsh."

"Harry's little wrongdoings turned into an international incident. I was a public example."

"I'm sorry. I didn't know. But I'm certain Harry must have had a good reason for disappearing. We don't always know why things happen."

"Lady, there was no good reason. Going to jail is bad. But there is no reason good enough for a man to lose his company and his reputation."

She reached out and laid her hand across his. The move was natural, meant to comfort, to reassure, to console. Except it didn't work out that way. There was a sizzle of instant awareness, a recognition of touch, as if he'd been waiting for her caress. Razor threaded his fingers through hers and released his breath in a rush.

Rachel looked past her guest, focusing on a spot beyond his left shoulder. Not looking directly at him seemed to relieve the overwhelming intensity of the pull she felt. Though she'd understood it, expected it, even waited for him to come, the reality of the man was far more disturbing than she'd ever imagined.

She felt the calluses on his hand, calluses that set off friction intensifying the flow of the peculiar feeling between them. "Trust me, Cody. Sometimes we have to believe, even when we don't understand. At first I didn't believe that I could trust Harry, either, but I was wrong."

"That's real comforting," Razor said, anger surging with swift unexpectedness as he responded to some unspoken communication in her touch. He started to stand. For a moment he almost whirled around and left the room.

The cat let out a low growl. A sudden touch of cold air curled across the back of Razor's neck, and

Rachel clasped his hand even more tightly, forcing him to sit.

"Now, see here, Rachel Kimble. I don't know what your—what Harry's game is, but I knew what kind of man Harry was when I came here, and learning that he's gone off and left his wife alone in this"—his eyes took in the peeling wallpaper and broken linoleum—"this broken-down old house doesn't change my opinion."

Rachel didn't hold back her amusement. A joyous laugh bubbled out, giving off a sound that sang like wind in Swiss chimes, light and melodious. "Oh, Cody, I'm not Harry's wife. Is that what you thought?"

"Certainly that's what I thought. He always referred to you as the beautiful Miss Rachel, the woman in his life. Who else would call a woman as young as you *Miss* Rachel, except a husband, a very *old* husband?"

"Harry is old all right, old-fashioned, a gentleman of the old school. He has certain standards that he insists we observe. I call him Uncle Harry, and because I'm an unmarried maiden, he calls me Miss Rachel."

"Harry's your uncle?" Razor didn't intend to allow his relief to show, but it did.

"Yes, Harry's my uncle, at least he says he is. I can't be positive about that, for I never knew my father had a brother. But then, I never knew my father at all. And the cards never told me about either him or Harry. That's very strange, you know. They told me you were coming."

"The cards told you about me?"

"Well, not by name of course. I never knew your name, but they did tell me about you."

The cat jumped down from the window and walked toward Razor as if to warn him against making any sudden moves.

"Look, Rachel," he began, "this doesn't make any sense. What cards?"

"These." With her free hand she held up a deck of playing cards. But they weren't like any playing cards Razor had ever seen. They were larger, and the pictures that adorned them were Medieval characters wearing bizarre costumes.

"Tarot cards," she explained.

"You're a fortune-teller?" The confusing picture suddenly seemed to right itself. What he was seeing was beginning to make sense. The black cat, the dark house with the strange lighting, the incense wafting from the fireplace, all for effect. "You thought I came to have my fortune told? Well, forget that, lady. I don't believe in such mumbo jumbo, and I make my own fortune."

Rachel let out a little sigh as she loosened his grip on her hand and shuffled the cards she was holding.

"No, I know you didn't come here for that. I know that you don't believe. That's all right. I didn't either—before."

"Before what?"

"It doesn't matter."

The cat growled again.

"I think Witchy would relax if you'd speak to her," Rachel said. "She isn't quite sure about you."

"The cat isn't sure. Hell, I'm not even sure. But you are?"

"More than ever. I'll show you." She continued to work the cards through her fingers until she finally selected a card and held it out for him to see. "Yes, I believe this card is you. Look at it and tell me what you see."

"Look, Rachel, I already told you that I don't believe in this fortune-telling stuff. But if these cards tell you things, just ask them where Harry is, and I'll get out of here!"

Brave words. Even as he spoke, Razor knew that he was trying to convince himself, not Miss Rachel Kimble. He'd been honest when he'd said that he didn't believe in fate, or Karma, or even love at first sight. Razor didn't believe in anything or anybody but himself, and he hadn't for a long time. He'd had his life under control and in order until Harry had come along. He couldn't begin to explain why he'd taken Harry in as a partner, or how he knew he wasn't going anywhere, not yet, not tonight.

"I don't know where Uncle Harry is, Cody. But if you ask the question, the cards might give you an answer. I never quite know what they'll say. But I promise, they will speak to you, if you're willing to go along."

Promise. So she did know where the old reprobate was. Razor didn't understand her game, but if he had to play along to find Harry, he would. At least for now.

"All right. But if you ever tell anybody that I let you do this, I'll deny it."

"No, you won't, Cody. You don't lie. Now, describe your card."

He took a look. "It's a Knight, like one of those from King Arthur's court. He's riding a white horse and carrying a sword. The sky is cloudy, windblown."

"What does he look like?"

It was eerie. The man on the card looked a little like him. "He's dark-haired and he has brown eyes." Well, his hair was dark, but he had gray eyes.

"And, like the knight, you're dashing and brave. You can be domineering, but you have a good heart. Now you must think what your question is to be."

"That's easy, where's Harry?"

She began to gather the cards together in a stack.

"I think there is a bigger question before you than Harry's location. You must shuffle the cards, Cody."

With a silent sigh of disbelief that he was continuing to take part, he separated the cards into two groups, fanned the large cards in his hand, and heard the sound of them slap against each other as he threaded the two stacks together.

"Now what? Do we play for matches, or do you have something more interesting in mind?"

She ignored him and made him feel silly for having injected a note of crude levity into what clearly was, for her, serious business.

"Now, Cody, cut the cards, three times to the left."

Once he'd complied, she gathered up the cards and reassembled them again, placing his Knight in the center of the table, faceup. She laid the top card over the Knight.

"This card covers you, Cody. Tell me what it is."

"What it is?"

"Yes. I've written labels at the bottom of each card. Read it to me."

He shrugged his shoulders and read, "The Two of Wands."

A slight smile curved her lips. "The Two of Wands means boldness and courage. You are about to embark on a new enterprise." She paused for a moment. "I'm afraid it also indicates that you have a proud but unforgiving nature."

"*Unforgiving* is the word here, and the new enterprise isn't through choice. What about my answer to the question where's Harry?"

"Be patient, Cody." She laid another card across the first two. "This card crosses you. This represents an obstacle to your new enterprise. What is it?"

Again he read the printed heading. "King of Pentacles. There's a guy sitting on a throne holding what looks like a Ninja weapon."

"It's a pentacle, a five-sided star, a magic symbol. Yes. The King could represent a chief of industry, a banker, or a businessman."

"Bankers. Businessmen. You're right about that. It'll take some kind of magic before they'll approve lending me any more money, ever again."

"Don't decide too quickly. Sometimes it takes time to understand the meaning of your cards."

"I'll bet."

The cat stood, turned around and around, then settled down again.

Rachel placed a card beneath the Knight's card, at the six o'clock position on a clock. "This is something that has already happened."

Cody described the card. "An upside-down Five

of Pentacles. And, boy, do these two people look sad."

"What do they look like to you, Cody?"

"I'd say they are two homeless people walking by a church in the snow. I guess this means that my past enterprise left me out in the cold."

"It might, but the card is upside down, which changes the meaning. It could signify a reversal of fortune."

"I'm for that." Cody realized he was actually enjoying their interchange. She'd been right about that pleasant, tickley feeling. Like warm brandy, it was still there in the pit of his stomach, its heat jarring him every now and then as their gazes met.

The coals were crackling as the fire died down. The cat had begun to purr softly, and Rachel, with the fireplace behind her, seemed to glow.

"Card four is behind you." She placed card four to the left of the Knight card, at nine o'clock. "And it is?"

"The Seven of Pentacles and it's right side up."

"I think this is a pause during the development of your new undertaking. Disappointment is passed away. There is the promise of success."

"I'm pausing all right. In fact my development has come to a full stop."

"At the top," she went on, "this card crowns you."

"I like this one. It shows a woman who looks like you, Rachel. She's wearing a Grecian dress. There's some kind of sign over her head. But the best part is that she's petting a lion. Does that mean you're going to turn me into a lamb?"

Rachel tried not to let her mind wander from what she was feeling. The meanings of the cards came to her with such clarity that she felt the energy in her fingertips. He didn't believe what she was saying, but that was all right. She hadn't believed either, until people started revealing the accuracy of her visions. What had started so many years ago as an act of schoolgirl rebellion had become her livelihood.

She went on. "The sign over her head is a sign of infinity. It stands for the cosmic state of eternal life. This is your essence, Razor Cody, the proud life spirit of a lion."

She laid out the next card at the three o'clock position. "This card is before you. It represents something that will happen, probably in the next few months."

"Well, this one is accurate, all right. Another upside-down card. It's the Eight of Cups. And it shows a man walking away. I think it's saying that I ought to get the hell out of here."

"No, it's upside down, remember. What it means is that you're abandoning the spiritual for the material, that you are bound to seek success, that you're about to find love."

"I like the sound of that, the success part anyway, but love? Not in this lifetime, lady. And I think you're wrong about the meaning. All those cups stacked up could mean that I'm going to get drunk enough to murder Harry when I find him. Is that it? When do I get my answer?"

"No, there's more." She laid a card down to the side of the others. "This is what you fear."

"More Cups. But this time it's a Nine."

Rachel held the card for a time, running her finger across it in troubled silence.

"What? Maybe we're going to have more tea?"

"You're not what you seem. Though you hunger for success, you fear it, Cody."

"Hell, I knew this was a bunch of baloney."

"Don't worry. You'll get what you want, but that's what you're afraid of. The second card will tell you more about your question. This represents the opinion of those around you."

"Cups again. This time a Two. Not much here. Oops, it's upside down as well. What does that tell me?"

She ducked her chin slightly and frowned. "I'm not sure. The card represents false love, violent passion, misunderstanding."

This time it was Cody who frowned. This time

he didn't give out with a quick quip. He felt a tightness inside his chest. False love and violent passion? He'd known that and he'd put it behind him long ago. At least he had until now. Suddenly he was a small boy again, watching his father with a woman, striking the woman, then walking away into the night and disappearing forever.

Rachel reached out and caught his hand again. "The last two cards will answer your question, Cody. Don't despair yet. The next card represents your hope." With one hand she exposed it. "What is it?"

"My Knight again, riding another horse, except this time it's the Knight of Pentacles."

"This represents trustworthiness, service, you're either about to find or leave—money?"

"That's exactly what I hope, that I'll find my money."

"Cody, I keep telling you, sometimes these things don't mean what you think they do."

"Turn them up, Miss Rachel. I'm liking this better and better."

She exposed the final card.

Razor gave out a low laugh. "Even I can recognize a Fool, Miss Rachel—an upside-down Fool."

"Folly," she said softly. "The Fool leads a merry chase."

Cody let go of Rachel's hand and leaned back in

the chair. "So, in the end I've been led on a merry chase. I could have saved you the trouble. I know that already."

He picked up the cup of blackberry tea, emptying it in a gulp, then absentmindedly set the cup on the shawl beside the saucer as he watched Rachel finger the exposed card and frown.

"So, the cards told you I was coming. They told you that I'd wait. Did they tell you what happens now?"

"Yes." She took a long, deep breath, then let it go. "They say that we will become lovers—and," she added in a rush, "that you're going to find a treasure."

"Lovers? You and I? I don't think so." But even as he said it, a vision came to him, a dizzying picture of her in his arms kissing him, her body moving against him, a vision so powerful that he felt himself harden in response.

"The cards can only speak, Cody, I don't control the answers."

At the moment he, too, was out of control. He felt his heart slam against his chest. The woman wasn't a fortune-teller, she was a sorceress, and he was deliberately being bewitched. He'd better find a way to stop the pounding, or he was in danger of being swept away by sensation.

"A treasure?" he said hoarsely, ignoring her first

statement. "And I believed *Harry* was full of it. It must be a family characteristic. You're doing it to me too."

"Doing what?"

"Seducing me with words, with spells. You're telling me that the cards announced my arrival and said we'd be lovers."

"The cards, and my visions."

Visions too. *Too* was the operative word here, *too* much, *too* bizarre, *too* unbelievable. Miss Rachel Kimble was beautiful. He could understand why Harry referred to her with such reverence. But there was something dangerous about her, mystical and dangerous.

That danger made Razor's gut twist and simmer with a slow, unalterable glow. For a moment, looking into the depths of those little-girl lavender eyes, he had an absurd yearning for summer meadows filled with bluebells and blue skies filled with clouds. Then his own vision returned; they were in his bed, making love.

Now who was the nut, the woman reading the cards or a recent ex-con contemplating lovemaking, bluebells, and clouds?

"You aren't going to give me the answers I need, are you?"

"I can only tell what is revealed to me," she

answered. "Would you like more tea? It's very calming."

"Tea? No, what I need is a bourbon and branch water."

"I'm sorry I don't have anything alcoholic. It isn't good for the psyche, but I'll get some tomorrow. Now, let me put away our cups, and I'll show you to your room." Rachel reached out for his cup and saucer.

Razor didn't know what was happening until it was over. She lifted the saucer, and as if the cup weren't sitting beside it, swept the cup to the floor in a crash.

"Oh . . ." she whispered. "I was concentrating so hard on the cards that I didn't know you'd put the cup there."

"But it was there in plain sight." At her panic-stricken look he amended his words to, "My fault," and started to pick up the pieces.

"Plain sight," he repeated under his breath. Razor looked up at the woman standing on the other side of the table and stopped. There was no mistaking the truth. He studied the eyes that looked at him in defiance—eyes that did not see.

"My God, you're blind!"

"Of course," she said softly. "I thought you knew."

TWO

The door to Razor's bedroom wouldn't close. Every time he closed the door, it immediately swung open again. Since his was the only room on the top floor, he finally left it ajar and went to bed.

Getting to sleep proved to be an impossibility. The floors creaked. Moss-laden tree limbs continually raked the outer walls. But more disturbing than that was his connection to the woman sleeping in the room below, and her suggestion that they would be lovers. Perhaps the vision wouldn't have been so strong if he'd heard the normal sounds of traffic, but the residents of the street closed their doors and pulled the quiet around them like a downy blanket.

When Razor finally drifted off, the cat was sitting on a chest at the end of his bed, her yellow eyes unblinking. The next morning she was still sitting in the same place. Razor could have sworn she hadn't moved. He couldn't say the same for himself.

For most of the night he'd tossed and turned and dreamed vivid dreams of a golden-haired woman etched in moonlight standing in his doorway, her lips curved into a half smile, her body draped in a flowing lavender robe. She'd start toward him, then just as she reached his bed, he'd wake and see the cat.

Once he was certain he'd heard someone coming up the stairs, someone big. But the steps died off midway, and silence settled in once more.

Now the sun was streaming through the blinds, making shadow bars across the bedclothes. "Damn! Bars!" Razor came to his feet. Though he'd only served a token sentence in a jail that had no bars, he never wanted any part of anything that made him think of prison again. When he turned around, the cat was gone.

The smell of coffee wafted up the stairs. There was no blackberry aroma this morning, no tea, just strong chicory coffee. Razor pulled on a pair of jeans, found his shaving kit, and made his way down to the ancient bathroom at the end of the corridor on the second floor.

The light switch beside the door brought no response. The bulb had burned out.

Razor looked around and shook his head. That crook. Harry had brought Rachel into this dump knowing that she couldn't see the disrepair. Razor hadn't had a good look around the previous night, but this morning the evidence was clear. Every moment he spent in Rachel's house, he found a reason to hammer another nail into Harry's coffin.

Razor unfolded the straight razor that had given him his nickname so many years ago and applied it to the shaving cream he'd smeared on his chin. It was the only thing he had left of his father and, defiantly, he'd learned to use it. Others used electric razors or the disposable kind he'd been forced to resort to while in jail, but with his heavy beard, the straight razor did a better job. He didn't need to see. He could get the job done in the dark.

As he wiped the cream on the jaunty yellow towel laid out for his use, he found himself making an imaginary list of the supplies he'd need to repair the house enough for him to live in some kind of comfort while he waited for Harry to appear.

Staying with Rachel was a necessity. He'd given up his condo, his offices, and his car. All that he owned was in the suitcase he'd thrown in the back of his battered pickup truck when he'd left New Orleans and headed to the Georgia coast.

He didn't intend to settle in, but for the time he was there, offering his building expertise in return for board was a fair exchange. Sharing her bed wasn't.

He pushed her out of his thoughts by continuing his mental shopping list. Light bulbs would be the first item. Then it came to him with a jolt: Burned-out light bulbs didn't matter to Rachel. That was probably why there was no porch light. Yet she'd had the lamp switched on over the table. But how did she know whether it was working properly? Because, he decided, the lamp hung down low enough so that she could feel its heat.

She could feel the lack of water pressure in the lavatory too. And she didn't have to see to know that the tiles in the floor were broken, that the wallpaper had a musty, mildewed odor, that the stairs creaked ominously, he realized as he walked down them. At some point, long ago, somebody else had recognized the potential danger of the swaying staircase and had installed the strange, ugly support post at the base.

In the daylight it seemed even more out of place, but the odd sensation beneath his fingertips had lessened. Razor paused for a moment to study the beam. If he wasn't mistaken, it was built of mahogany, which didn't match the rest of the staircase. But it was far from new, so the structural problems with the house must date back to its construction.

Curiously Razor ran his fingers along the front. Scars in the wood. At some point there had been an attachment, perhaps some ornate carving along the lower part. When the beam had been installed, no attempt had been made to sand the surface. That made the support purely functional, not decorative. No wonder this house had been allowed to deteriorate rather than be chosen for restoration like its neighbors.

It was a lemon.

Harry had bought a lemon and installed Miss Rachel in it, knowing that she couldn't see its sorry state.

That and the payback Harry was due for bringing Razor into the life of a lonely woman who believed in Knights and lovers was even more reason to render Harry bald.

He wasn't going to live there, he decided. Harry had already cost him enough money. This house wasn't his problem. He'd started many years ago as a carpenter, but restoring antique houses wasn't where he'd made his fortune—his recently lost fortune.

Just simple, reasonable repairs would be enough. There was no way he'd use the money he'd salvaged to put this monstrosity back in the condition of the other houses on the street. The money he'd collected on an old debt wouldn't have paid his fine, but it would support him for a time, providing he lived frugally. He hadn't counted on having to wait for Harry, but he would, and if it became necessary, he'd find another place to stay. Razor entered the kitchen, putting all thoughts of the house out of his kind. No point in letting Rachel know what he knew about Harry's mean-spirited gesture.

"Harry's motives are yet to be decided, Cody."

Razor jerked his eyes toward the woman who was shaking her head at him in reproof. Had he spoken aloud again?

The cat meowed and jumped to the windowseat, eyeing Razor threateningly. She meowed again, a shrill, demanding cry.

"She's waiting for you to greet her, Cody. Her name is Witchy."

"Figures. Does she cast spells in your behalf?"

"I don't know. Do you think she does?"

"I don't think you need any help."

"Did you sleep well?" she asked, then answered her own question with a no. She'd heard him tossing through the night. Once she'd even been drawn to his room, just to reassure him. She'd walked to the bed and touched his bare shoulder. He'd grown quiet. Then she was the one who tossed for the rest of the night.

"No," he echoed, "which is unusual. I can sleep anywhere. I think it was the cat. She shared my room."

"Have some French toast, Cody. We have some nice blackberry syrup to douse it in."

"I don't eat French toast. But I'll take some eggs and bacon."

"Sorry, I don't have any bacon, and I used all the eggs. I'll add them to my shopping list."

Rachel turned and carried a butter-yellow plate to the same table that had been covered with the pink shawl the previous night. This morning it was draped with a square of yellow-and-white fabric.

"Sit down, Cody. I've made coffee."

The coffee he could deal with, not the piece of toast cut into a circle complete with a smiley face drawn in with blackberries.

"Where's yours?" he asked as he sat.

"Oh, I've already eaten."

Razor glanced around the kitchen. If she'd already eaten, she'd washed the dishes and put them away. She might have convinced him if he hadn't spied the single eggshell in a cat-embossed garbage can by the refrigerator. The one eggshell—not two. He didn't know much about making French toast, but he did know it was a good way to stretch one egg and two pieces of stale bread into looking like more. He recognized what she'd done because his mother had been good at that kind of logic.

Razor ate the toast and drank the coffee. To do otherwise would let her know what he'd observed, and she was already uncannily perceptive about his thoughts.

"I do my shopping today," she said quietly. "Monday they have the best bargains on what is left from the weekend. I'll get bacon and eggs then. Don't worry, Razor, even though I'm blind, I read tarot cards, blend tea, and make ceramics to pay my bills. I manage."

It was uncanny how she knew what he was thinking, and unnerving as well. He wondered if she knew about his dreams, wondered, then caught sight of the blush on her face and forced them from his mind. She knew. Maybe she'd sent that cat to torment him. Razor was beginning to believe that there *was* more of a purpose to his coming there than just waiting for Harry.

"I'm sure you manage fine, but since today is shopping day, Miss Rachel, I think I'll come with you. If I'm destined to wait for Harry, I'll need to lay in supplies. I expect to pay my way."

He wondered how much it would cost to build a wall around his mind, a wall that would keep him from thinking about them as lovers.

"Don't worry, Cody. You're safe," she said as if she understood his fears. "I may have misunderstood what I was seeing."

"Does that happen often?"

"Not often, but sometimes. As for your accompanying me, that will be nice. I usually go alone."

"Is that safe? I'd think you'd have someone with you."

"I've never had anyone with me, Razor. I always liked it that way. Shall we go early, before the heat gets too bad?"

"Why not? Where is the nearest supermarket?"

"Oh, I don't go to the supermarket. I shop at the little neighborhood market down the street past the park. Mr. Grossman knows me. He looks after me."

"But wouldn't you get better prices at a supermarket?"

"Probably, but cheap isn't always best for someone like me. Besides, for that I'd need a car."

"I'm sorry," he said, allowing himself to really look at her for the first time since he'd entered the kitchen. She was wearing a loose-fitting denim dress over a T-shirt that had the tip of a furry cat's ears peeking out through the half-buttoned top. She'd caught her hair in some kind of clamp that allowed it to cascade down her back. She wasn't wearing makeup, except for a light touch of lip gloss. Razor had the absurd feeling that she looked like a wife, a happy wife, and he filled his mouth with coffee to keep himself from kissing her good morning.

"I don't mind walking. It keeps me from depending on others. People who live here say that it's hard to drive out to the malls and get back, with the one-way streets."

"Tell me about that. I drove around for an hour before a cop decided I must either be a drunk or a crook casing the area. When he found out I was lost, he was kind enough to lead me to your door. With the river and all these special parks and squares it's like being in a maze."

"Where'd you park?"

"In the alley behind your house. I hope you don't mind."

"It's called a lane, and I don't mind."

Rachel felt Razor's eyes on her. She could sense his guarded interest, his tightly concealed emotions. She'd felt them for most of the night, felt them and not known what to do. She couldn't explain, for she didn't fully understand. All she knew was that he was making everything so hard when it wasn't necessary. He'd have to learn acceptance, just as she had, and until that time she'd be patient.

She'd thought she was prepared for his coming, for what that would mean to her. But there were emotions swirling through her that she didn't understand: anticipation and fear. She'd thought she'd have more time. Only now was she learning to live without her eyes, learning to rely on her senses and the outside power of something akin to second sight that seemed to be growing with every hour. Now *he* had arrived, and it would all end. The only thing she didn't know was how and when.

Witchy jumped down and padded over to her, rubbing her ankles and making that comforting little purr that Rachel had come to understand was Witchy's own kind of cat reassurance.

"While you're finishing your breakfast, I'll get my list."

"List?"

"Of course, I can't see, but I can still write. It makes it easier for Mr. Grossman if he knows what I need."

A fresh surge of anger swept over Razor. How dare Harry abandon this woman for strangers to see to her needs? How dare he install her in this falling-down piece of junk and disappear?

"He cares about me, Razor," she said softly as she left the room. "You don't understand, but it's true. And I'm very grateful. When he found me, I was in a school that taught me how to live with my blindness, a place without open doors. And there was nobody to take me anywhere. This house isn't much, but it's mine, at least for now."

After she'd left the room, he replayed her conversation. He wasn't psychic, but he could read the inferences in her voice and determine that the words *at least for now* meant that change was more probable than possible. And she'd said she was learning to live with her blindness. That meant she hadn't always been blind.

Moments later they were walking down a street lined with gnarled old live oaks, bedecked with swatches of gray moss, clinging defiantly to the bent limbs angled to the ground. Leaves, golden and red, crunched beneath their feet. She walked slowly without faltering, as if she were following some kind of invisible line. Razor couldn't help but notice the restored row houses along her street, all two-story with neat little verandas and colorful exteriors. Only Rachel's house was in such a state of disrepair.

"Harry intends to fix it up, Cody. He only bought this house because it was cheap and he knew I wouldn't mind waiting."

"Rachel, knowing the way Harry operates, you may not live long enough to get your house fixed up. I can understand why it was cheap. It's falling down. The question is why, if these others have been kept up, was this one allowed to deteriorate?"

"It's been through several owners who planned to restore it, but after beginning they changed their minds. I understand the house was used for a school forty years ago. Since then nobody seemed to want to live in it permanently."

"Why? Why would this house be singled out and abandoned?"

"I think it's because of the Captain. You see, it's supposed to be haunted."

"I can believe that. Who's the Captain?"

"Captain R. B. Perine. He was a very successful pirate. But he'd given up his pillaging and plundering, built this house, and sailed to England, where he'd expected to be married. His fiancée broke their engagement, and on his voyage home he was caught in a storm. The Captain went down with his ship. There are those who say his ghost comes back to check on his treasure."

"So, you tell fortunes to make a living. You have visions that predict the future, and you live in a haunted house? I don't know why I ever thought that Harry was a mystery."

"Harry is a mystery. So is the Captain. But I don't mind. In fact I like to think they're looking after me."

"You share your house with a witch cat and a ghost and you like it?"

"I think it's because I understand the house. We're both flawed. That makes us fit together very well. And now you're here to help me protect it."

"We? What's this *we* stuff?" Now they were getting down to it. Harry had bought the house, made certain that Razor knew how to find it, and lit out. How Rachel's special powers fit into Harry's scheme didn't make sense. It was all too confusing.

Rachel stumbled slightly, and Razor's arm went out to steady her. When she moved on, it seemed only reasonable that he continue to hold on to her. Reasonable and right.

He cleared his throat to conceal the shiver that swept over him.

"Don't worry, Cody. Everything will work out fine. Trust me. I have two clients this afternoon. While I take care of them, you can go to the mall and buy what's on your list. Then tonight we'll have a nice dinner and talk."

"My list? How do you know about my list? I haven't even made one."

"Oh, didn't you mention it? I was sure you did."

They stopped at the corner and after a moment Rachel started across the intersection and into the park that was planted right in the middle of the street.

"Rachel, good morning." A woman walking her poodle met them and paused, glaring at Razor suspiciously. "Going to Grossman's?"

"Yes, Maude. I'm so glad you're out. I'd like you to meet Razor Cody. He'll be staying with me for a while. Razor, this is my friend Maude."

"Oh?" Maude drew the *oh* out into an unmistakable question.

"Don't worry, Maude. Harry sent him."

"Well, I don't know how good a recommendation that is," Maude replied.

Razor grinned at Maude. He liked her already. He liked anybody who showed a healthy skepticism about Harry.

"But having a boarder will show the city council that you'll have an income to begin repairs on your house," Maude went on. "It should make them happier about granting another extension on your restoration time."

"Cody, Maude sells my ceramic cats and my special tea mixes in her little shop on Riverwalk."

Oblivious to the shrill yapping of the dog, Maude was still eyeing Razor with a certain amount of censure, which, since Rachel couldn't see, Maude didn't bother to hide.

"He's all right, Maude," Rachel said reassuringly, "really. I've been expecting him. Stop barking, Petey. Be nice to Mr. Cody, he's very important to me."

The dog hushed and sat, staring at Razor with curiosity. Then he began to wag his tail.

"Well, then . . . if you're sure." Maude gave Razor a final glare of warning and moved past, the little poodle tugging at its leash in an effort to get to Rachel, who leaned down to pet him.

As they moved away, Razor tried to recapture the odd sense of warmth they'd enjoyed before they'd been stopped, but now he was uncomfortable. Maude's words having to do with convincing the city council that she could make repairs and thus get extension on her restoration time, stayed with him "Exactly how long have you been here, Rachel?"

"Nine months. I came here in January, when the wind from the river is cold and the trees shiver."

"I thought Savannah was the city of sunshine and flowers," Razor said.

"Oh, it is. You should be here in April, when the azaleas are in full bloom. It's beautiful then."

"Then you hadn't lost your eyesight when you came?"

"Oh, yes. I've been blind for nearly two years. But I knew. I could smell them, and in my mind's eye I could see the blossoms. There's a park here, especially for the blind where we can touch and smell the flowers."

"Touch and smell I can deal with, but mind's eye? I'm afraid I don't understand."

"Neither do I, Cody. But when I lost my vision, I seemed to gain a special kind of sight. I see things and I know things."

The man cleaning the leaves from beneath the wrought-iron benches placed along the walks greeted them, and a car horn honked and the driver waved. That someone would wave at Rachel when she couldn't see seemed strange to Razor. What was even stranger was watching Rachel return the wave.

"Does everybody in Savannah know you?"

"Oh, no. Of course I do have friends here. That seems odd to me. I never had friends before I lost my vision. Now that I can't see them, people seek me out."

Somewhere along the way Razor's fingers had moved, and now they were holding hands. She smiled, and suddenly there seemed to be a kind of lilt in her step. Razor loosened his grip. What was he doing, acting like some kid taking his girl for a walk? He was out for revenge, not some kind of regression to his high school years.

"What's wrong with stopping to smell the roses, Cody? You never know when you'll lose your sense of smell."

"Rachel, you may have some remarkable kind of extrasensory perception, but you can't possibly understand how wrong it is of you to see me as some kind of—of—"

"Knight on a white horse? But you are. Remember the tarot card?"

"You may see me as a white knight, but I think of myself as more of a bounty hunter, a mean, angry bounty hunter."

"Nonsense. You're a good man."

"I'm a . . ." What he was was a sexually aroused man, a man who couldn't keep his hands off this woman. "A driven man. I've been called unfeeling. I've been called cold, and several ladies I've known briefly have called me worse. But it's been a long time since anybody called me good."

"Well, I don't believe all that for one minute. You're special, and even if you are here only temporarily, we're going to be good together. I'm sure of that."

Razor groaned as he felt that little shimmer of heat run up his arm and race to his groin. It didn't feel good. It was more like a jab of reproach. It said "stay away" at the same time that his body cued up in anticipation. She was right about being good together. Suddenly his own mind's eye was filled with that recurring vision of her face pressed against his chest, of her lips parted, waiting. His pulse raced.

"I don't think," he snapped, "that being together is a good idea. I don't know what your visions are telling you, but I keep telling you that I'm only here for revenge, Rachel. Then I'm gone, and I don't want to hurt you in the process."

"One thing I've learned in the last two years is that sometimes we have to hurt to appreciate what we have. Only pain brings growth."

"You sound like my mother."

"Did she hurt too?"

Razor didn't want to answer that question. He tried never to look back, never to relive his mother's pain. She hadn't cried when his father had left, nor during the terrible times when her suffering must have been excruciating. For the most part he'd been successful in forgetting. He had never discussed his past with anyone.

"For five years," he heard himself saying in a low voice, "until she died. But she never complained. To her every day was a gift. She had cancer, the slow, painful, killing kind. I never understood how she could stand the pain. I couldn't have. I wished that she would die."

"How old were you?"

"Seventeen. She wanted to see me finish high school. Graduation was on Saturday. She died the next day."

"I'm so sorry, Razor." Rachel stopped and slid her arm around his waist, pressing her face against his chest. She held him for a moment, then lifted her head, her lips parted in anticipation.

Just as he'd visualized moments earlier.

He ran his thumb across her chin, then, without a thought, lowered his face, allowing their lips to touch. She had time to pull away. He could have stopped. But neither did. Instead they seemed to melt against each other. And there, in the sunshine, in the park, Razor Cody kissed Miss Rachel Kimble.

The taste and the warm feel of her erased any thought of restraint. The kiss deepened, and he heard her make a little sound of pleasure. His mind accepted what it had fought through most of the night; he wanted this woman; they were right together.

Then, to his surprise, she was dragging her mouth away. "Oh, Razor," she whispered. "I knew it would be like this."

He felt as if he were waking up from a deep sleep. He held on to her shoulders, protesting her movement, until he opened his eyes and saw her smile of satisfaction.

No! This couldn't be happening. He had to get hold of himself. Razor Cody wasn't a man to give in to daydreams or pretense. He didn't share any part of himself with anyone. He was a man in control of his life, at least he had been before Harry, before Harry's decision to cut costs on a job had brought disaster. Before he ran into a woman who thought she was waiting for him. Razor had to put an end to this madness.

But he took another look at the sweetness in her face and knew that he couldn't hurt someone as vulnerable as his mother had been. He couldn't hurt Rachel. This wasn't her fault. "I'm sorry," he found himself explaining, chasing the hardness from his voice. "I shouldn't have done that. I don't want to hurt you. I've seen enough pain in my life."

"You're thinking of your mother. I understand. There were times when I wanted to die too."

Yes, he was thinking of his mother's pain, and he was thinking about Rachel. He'd tried to pull away, but she was still holding him. There was a smell of wildflowers in her hair, and a trace of moisture on her cheeks. She was crying for him, sharing a stranger's pain.

A bird chattered shrilly, breaking the comforting moment. Without speaking, Rachel started across the square.

"I'll take you to see the Minis house one day," she said as if nothing out of the ordinary had happened. "It's just down this street. You'll like it. At least you will appreciate what the previous owner did."

Razor followed her, still jarred by what had happened and grateful for the change of subject. "How's that?"

"Well, since you're a builder, you probably know more about codes than I do."

"Not about building restoration."

"In the Historic District," Rachel went on, "the city has enacted restrictions on the refurbishing of these houses. Plans must meet their approval, and we must use certain colors and comply with all sorts of regulations, including the time allowed to complete the job. Mr. Minis didn't want to follow their wishes."

"Now he's the *former* owner? Pretty stiff penalty for not conforming."

"Oh, they didn't kill him off or anything. He went from natural causes, but before he died, he got even. He covered all the windows with heavy plywood, then, using the proper colors and the proper designs, he painted beautiful Victorian murals on the wood. They won, but so did he."

"A man after my own heart. So, what are they doing to the house?"

"The new owner is restoring it according to the code. But I think that there are some who'll be sorry to see the murals go."

"You?"

"I don't know. I never saw them, so I can't be sure how they looked."

"But I thought you could see things in your mind's eye."

"Not everything. And what I see only applies to people, people I connect with. That's why, when I read the tarot cards, I have to have you describe the card for me. I just pass on the information that applies to each card. My special vision allows me to see things that touch my life, but not necessarily others'."

People I connect with. She was right. Even Razor

could identify the connection between them, and Rachel had given him ample evidence of her ability to become one with his thoughts.

"Are there any more renegades around?"

"Well, there is the Juliette Gordon Low house to your right at the end of Lafayette Square. It's the pink house you can see through the trees. She started the Girl Scouts of America. It's their museum now. Would you like to see it? We could get the groceries later. But I have to get back by two o'clock."

"To see the two clients you'd mentioned?"

"That's right. I'm doing readings for them—the tarot cards. We could see the Girl Scouts Museum now and get the groceries later."

"No, scouting was never my cup of tea. Excuse me, no pun intended."

"None taken. I've created a special tea in her honor. I call it the Juliette."

Razor felt a growing respect for Rachel's ability to look after herself. He'd never thought much about tea, but somehow the mystery fit this woman.

"The architecture is supposed to be very nice," she was saying. "Maude says they have a doorway just like the one in her house. But the Low house's doorframe has been restored, and Maude's is about to fall down. I don't suppose you would—"

"No, I wouldn't," he snapped, trying to divorce

himself from any suggestions that he participate further. "I'm not going to get involved in restoring anything. My trip to Savannah is purely for the purpose of finding Harry."

"I don't believe that for one minute," Rachel said as they came to the sidewalk and walked to the light. "And neither do you. Mr. Grossman's store is on the opposite corner."

The way she switched from the mysticism of her special visions to the reality of life kept him shaken. He didn't know how to deal with the mystery, so he focused on the reality.

"And you come here alone to shop? Shouldn't you have a white cane or a dog or something?"

"I have a cane. I didn't bring it since you're with me. I'd like to have a dog, but they're very expensive, and I know that I won't need one forever. It seemed wrong to take an animal that should go to someone who'd need him for a long time."

The light changed, and at Razor's urging they started across.

"What do you mean, you won't need one forever?"

Rachel counted her steps, stepping up on the curb at exactly the right time. How much to tell Cody? She wasn't sure. But she had never lied; she wouldn't know how.

"My blindness isn't supposed to be permanent.

The doctors told me that my sight could come back at any time."

"But it hasn't yet."

"No, but now I know it will."

"More of that mind's-eye business?"

"Yes."

He would have asked more, except that he didn't think he wanted to know, and they'd reached the store. A thin, bespectacled man was out the door before Razor could open it.

"Rachel, I've been watching for you. How are you today?"

"I'm fine, Mr. Grossman. I'd like you to meet my new . . . boarder, Mr. Cody."

"Boarder?" The grocery owner studied Rachel shrewdly. "Have you talked to Maude about this?"

"Yes, she met him this morning in the park. Razor's a builder. He's going to look at Maude's doorframe."

"Oh, then that's fine." Mr. Grossman shook Razor's hand vigorously. "Can't be too careful about who you let in. But if he's going to help you get started on the house, that makes it all right."

That was the second reference Razor had heard about Rachel's house. He was getting a bad feeling. Now she'd committed him to looking at Maude's doorframe. If he didn't do it, Razor had the feeling that Mr. Grossman and Rachel's care committee would come in the dead of night and string him up from one of those trees in the park.

Miraculously Rachel's list was filled, not with bruised leftovers as Mr. Grossman was apologetically insisting, but with the finest produce and meats in his case. By the time Razor finished adding his selections, it was clear that they weren't going to carry it all home in their arms. Razor arranged to take the supplies Rachel needed immediately and come back in the truck for the rest.

With each of them carrying one bag, they started back to Rachel's house. He was glad he had his arms full, otherwise, they'd have found their way back around Rachel. This time it was Razor who did the questioning.

"These clients you have this afternoon, who are they and why do they come to you?"

"One is a friend who operates a local bookstore. She carries all sorts of wonderful New Age materials. Occasionally I go into her store and give readings. She's been having a bit of a problem with the man she's in love with. She comes to me privately, for reassurance."

"And you read the tarot cards. Don't you ever worry about what you're telling these people? I mean, what if you're wrong?"

"But I never am. Besides, I only say what the cards say. I've studied very hard to learn all I can possibly know about the cards, and I only tell what they reveal. Every client has to decide for him or herself how the answers apply to their lives."

And you decided that we'd be lovers? He choked back that question, asking instead, "Who's the other client?"

"He's new. A historian doing some research on Savannah. I don't know him very well yet, but we get on nicely."

"He? You allow a perfect stranger inside your house?"

Rachel laughed. "I thought we'd already covered that. Besides, until I feel comfortable with the way a person accepts my reading, I never tell him everything I see."

They moved through the park, stopped on the sidewalk that ran alongside it, and crossed the street. Razor wondered what she'd kept back in his reading. Then he shook himself. How the hell had he gotten into such a muddle? He was on the verge of believing all this nonsense.

Believing that she'd been expecting him.

Believing that she believed he was some kind of knight charging to her rescue.

"What *didn't* you tell me?" he asked.

Rachel stopped and shifted her grocery bag to the other arm as if she thought she might need a shield between them.

"What, Rachel?"

Should she tell him the truth or wait? The decision was hard.

She took a deep breath and answered.

"I didn't tell you that you'd bring back my sight."

THREE

"How do you know about Captain Perine?" Razor asked, and pushed his empty plate away so that he could prop his elbows on the table and watch Rachel as she talked.

He found himself doing that often. There was a way she had of turning her head as if she were hearing her answers come through the air. She wore a half smile of approval that parted her lips and made him want to touch them with his own.

He'd returned from his trip to the home-repair center in the shopping strip at the outskirts of town and unloaded his supplies at the back door, leaving his truck parked beneath a back porch built high enough off the ground to allow him to do so. Gathering up the groceries, he'd climbed the steps and entered the kitchen, where he'd found Rachel stirring a pot of something that smelled very good.

"Did you have any trouble getting back?" she'd asked.

"Not this time. I'm beginning to figure out the one-way streets. I've never driven in a city where a street ended at a park square and picked up on the other side and the only way you can turn takes you the wrong way."

"At least it keeps down the traffic. There aren't any shortcuts through the Historic District. Are you hungry?"

"Very. How did your sessions go?"

"Quite well. Helen, my friend who owns the bookstore, has decided to break off with the man she's been seeing. It's the new client who is proving to be interesting."

"The historian?"

"He claims to be a historian, but I think he's really looking for treasure. He's convinced there must be all kinds of hidden fortunes in the walls and on the grounds of these old houses."

"Why would there be treasure here?"

"He says that starting with the threat of Indian attacks, the Revolutionary War, and on through the War Between the States, people hid their valuables."

"And have you sensed any?"

"No, at least not that I'm aware of. My sight doesn't extend to objects, only people, emotions.

But sometimes sensations come that can't be defined. I might be touching a treasure and think my awareness is coming from someone in the house next door."

"But I've heard about people who have the ability to find lost objects."

"Yes, but I don't seem to have that kind of power. I told him that he ought to be consulting a psychic. But he isn't convinced."

Razor frowned. Rachel might have more extrasensory perception than she knew. He didn't want her placed in any danger. But if someone thought she could lead them to a treasure, her special gift might be invaluable.

The thought stayed with him all through their evening meal, that knowledge and the memory of their kiss. He tried unsuccessfully to forget about her startling statement that they'd become lovers. None of it made any sense, unless she were part of Harry's escape plot. Then there was the prediction that he'd bring back her sight.

Razor was no fairy godmother, and he didn't believe in miracles. This time her cards and her visions were wrong.

The pot Rachel had been stirring contained a seafood gumbo, prepared as well as any he'd eaten in New Orleans. She'd served the meal with slow, deft motions that seemed as natural as any woman might display in her kitchen.

They were sitting at the same intimate little table with its bright cover and overhead lamp. It didn't take Razor long to know that this room was where she lived, the heart of the house. Somehow, in the early evening shadows, under the pink lampshade, the shabbiness of the house seemed to lessen.

Razor tried to pry his gaze away from her lavender eyes. He supposed someone else might call them blue, but something about the lively intensity of her interest deepened the color and turned them to a subtle shade somewhere between orchid and amethyst.

At least he didn't have to conceal his interest, nor its resulting effect on his body. That would have been a problem, for he couldn't seem to keep his eyes off her. Hell, he'd admitted that she was beautiful, but it was her innocent serenity that drew him into her spell.

He'd always considered himself a practical man, not given to fantasies or impossible dreams. He couldn't account for his interest in Rachel. But he recognized his growing attraction. The choices were clear; he could walk away and forget about Harry, start over, get on with his life. Or he could stay and finish what he'd started.

Leaving would be the smart choice. Rachel

wasn't his responsibility. He'd been attracted to women before, and once he'd slept with them, the interest had vanished. As he saw it, he either had to sleep with Rachel or treat her the way a protective older brother might.

And if he told himself that his feelings were that of a brother, he'd be as big a liar as Harry. Of course he was attracted to her, physically and more. There was a kind of super-kinetic link between them that was intensifying with every moment they were together.

Even she'd known that, giving voice to the need by saying that they'd be good together. So, he'd admit that he was attracted to her, that he'd like to take her to bed and touch every part of her, but he had no intention of taking his desire any farther than the erotic dreams he'd had. Rachel wasn't a mutual-convenience kind of woman, a woman he could share a bed with and leave behind when he'd settled with Harry.

Razor had seen his father take off without a moment's thought for his wife and child. His mother had never totally recovered from that abandonment, and Razor had sworn never to follow in his father's footsteps. After his mother died, he'd become a loner, never allowing himself to feel anything for anybody. It had been his means of protection, of survival. And he'd traveled alone. Until now.

Dammit, he was out for revenge, not romance. In spite of what she said, Miss Rachel Kimble would want things he couldn't promise her, like marriage and forever.

"I'm not asking you for anything you aren't prepared to give, Cody," she said in a whisper, and reached out, her fingertips grazing his knuckles as he jerked his hand away in acknowledgment of the heat that arced between them. "And I won't—ever. Just let what is to happen, happen."

He'd already done that. He'd kissed her. She didn't have to ask. He might not have her second sight, but he recognized commitment when it touched him. And Rachel was doing more than touching. She was wrapping him up in desire and sealing the wrap with her trust.

"Tell me about your ghosts," he said in a hoarse voice.

"All right." She drew her hand back and placed it in her lap. It took all his concentration not to go after her hand and capture it with his. Every time she touched him, his desire grew—and his confusion.

"Captain Perine isn't the only ghost around," she said. "That's what I love about this city. Savannah is alive with spirits. Practically every house has its own private resident, sometimes more than one.

There are nice ones, like the lovely old lady who stands in the shadows of the garden at the Owens-Thomas house. She wears an antebellum gown that smells of lemon."

"What does she do, haunt the tree frogs?"

"No, she's supposed to be waiting for a carriage, a carriage that never comes. Some of the ghosts are children, some slaves. Our most famous ghost is Captain Flint who haunts the Pirate House."

"What's the Pirate House?"

"It's an old seaman's inn where notorious eighteenth-century pirates drank rum with sailers from the trading ships. Innocent men were often shanghaied and woke up to find themselves on the seas bound for some foreign land. According to the old-timers, you can still hear Flint moaning on his deathbed, shouting for rum and cursing those who stole his treasure."

"Tell me about *our* pirate."

"Captain Perine was a bit of a mystery. He had his own ship and he was wealthy. Not much was known about his business, but people described him as a towering man who stood over six feet tall. With his red-orange hair and full beard, people were intimidated by his appearance even before they heard the rumors of his being a pirate. That's what made him so successful in his work."

Red-orange hair and beard? This time there was

no mistaking the breath of cold air that swept over Razor. He considered Rachel's description before voicing his next question. "Rachel, what does Harry look like?"

"Look like?" she repeated quizzically, then took her time before she answered. "I don't know. I never knew Harry until after I was blind."

"But surely, in some of your visions, or that special power you have—"

"No. Oddly enough, Harry is a complete blank. I've never understood that. The only person I ever saw was you."

Razor was beginning to understand more than he wanted to know. The whole idea was too bizarre. "How did you two meet?"

"He came to me in Atlanta, at the Center for the Blind where I'd been sent after I left the hospital."

"Hospital? You never said anything about a hospital. Why were you there? What happened to you, Rachel?"

"I was . . . beaten. An old woman was being mugged in the park, and I tried to stop it. The gang turned on me. I don't remember much about it, but I was near death in a coma for a time. When I finally came to, I was blind. The doctors say my sight could eventually come back. But it hasn't, not yet."

Razor sucked in a ragged breath. He didn't have to have one of Rachel's visions to see what she'd described. That anyone could have turned on her was beyond belief. That she would disregard her own safety to help someone else wasn't. He allowed his vision of what happened to go one step farther. "Did they—?"

"No, Cody. They didn't rape me. They might have, but someone came, a jogger with a dog. He frightened them away."

"And the old woman?"

Rachel let out a dry laugh. "Who knows? She apparently ran away. When the jogger found me, I was alone."

"But wasn't there anyone to help you? A mother? A sister?"

"I'm an orphan. At least I thought I was, until Harry came. He found me just at the right time."

"Maybe if he'd found you earlier, you wouldn't have been in a park alone with a gang of muggers. What were you doing there anyway?"

"I often walked in the park. I'd go there to sketch. Nobody had ever hurt me there before."

"I know that life's a—" He swallowed the word *bitch* and tried to think of an acceptable replacement. But all he could think about was that she'd been hurt last by Harry, who had promised her safety and had left her here alone. The louse.

"No, Cody. Don't think like that. I had to leave the center and I had nowhere to go. My job as a nursery-school teacher was gone. I couldn't look after myself. I had no money. Then Harry came and brought me here."

"And you never saw what he looked like."

"No. Why, is that important?"

"I guess not." Razor couldn't bring himself to say that Harry was an intimidating man, over six feet tall. He didn't even want to think about it. It was too strange, too unreal.

Instead he asked, "What does the *R. B.* stand for in our pirate's name?"

"I don't know."

But Razor did. He didn't have to have the gift of sight. The *R* stood for *red* and the *B* for *beard.* Redbeard. A man with a bushy red-orange beard and strange-looking hair. Just like Harry's.

As they washed and put away the dishes, Rachel tried to understand the rush of confusing emotions that churned inside her head and stomach. She'd seen Cody's arrival and understood that his coming in some way signaled an end to her blindness. The tarot cards had predicted that he'd take a lover, and she'd assumed that it was her. Perhaps she'd assumed too much.

She'd always known that he was in the light at the end of her tunnel. She'd recognized his voice, his presence, instantly, but beyond that her special sight didn't go.

Rachel had always read the tarot cards for others. A true psychic didn't read her own fate. Except for once, when she'd carefully pulled one card from the deck and laid it aside until Maude could identify it. She'd chosen the Knight on his horse, in the storm. After she'd come to Savannah, her second sight had become even stronger, and she'd become proficient enough with the cards to mystify her friends with her accuracy.

Since she'd been in her little house, she'd come to accept the intensification of her strange gift and the use she was able to make of it. In a city that loved its ghosts, her talent was welcomed as just another of the little touches that made the Historic District so special. And the residents embraced Rachel and protected her as one of their own. She'd lost her past and found her future.

But none of her visions went far enough. There was a kind of blank void at the end of her joy. Was she right to believe that her sight would return? Once it did, what would she do? She'd taken classes part-time, when she could, given her hand-to-mouth existence. But she hadn't completed her degree, and a nursery-school teacher who couldn't even look after herself certainly couldn't care for children. She'd never made any money from her art.

Now she'd have to start again, here, for Savannah, she knew, was where she belonged, whether or not Cody remained.

Without Harry's confidence in her Rachel wasn't sure she could do it. Razor didn't have to tell her how run-down her house was. The city council had explained that vividly when they'd given her an extension on her six-month limit to begin repairs.

Rachel sighed. Even with insurmountable problems ahead she'd become foolishly accepting of her situation, content to wait. The past was gone, as was her previous life. The house liked her and she liked it, just as it was. The thought of change was unsettling. She'd grown accustomed to her blindness, and in some strange way it was her protection. She was safe. Even in her state of constant uncertainty there was a feeling of order about her life. Giving that up was frightening.

She liked standing at the sink next to Cody, washing a dish, rinsing it, and handing it to him to be dried and put away. She wasn't sure she wanted anything to be different. And because she couldn't see the light at the end of the tunnel, she didn't know whether Cody would be there to share it.

"Where have you lived before, Cody?"

"My business was in New Orleans. And I do mean *was*. Except for my tool chest, it's gone now, every nail and saw, every piece of equipment. The police didn't escort me to the city limits, but they made it very clear that my welcome mat had been withdrawn."

"Are you going to tell me what happened between you and Harry?"

"Why not? You deserve to know something about your loving uncle. He's a crook. He wormed his way into my company with the promise of a huge contract at a time I needed work to keep my men busy. He was willing to merge his business with mine because his firm wasn't big enough to handle the job."

"That sounds like Harry, always willing to share what he has."

"Ha! He failed to tell me that this huge contract was his means of destroying one of the biggest crooks in New Orleans. From the very beginning he intended to sabotage the hotel we were building, and he did. And me with it."

"I don't believe he intended to hurt you. That doesn't sound like the man I know."

"Believe it. He ordered inferior supplies and bribed the inspectors. Then he waited until the gentleman in question was hosting a party for business associates, knowing that the balcony around the hotel atrium would collapse."

Rachel gasped, allowing the dish she was holding

to slide into the water. "I don't believe Harry would allow anyone to get hurt."

"Oh, he didn't. Just before the balcony fell, he called in a bomb threat, emptying the building. It was the weight of the scaffolding he'd erected to provide special seating for his guests to view the entertainment in the atrium below that did it. There wasn't a soul in the building when it fell. Only about a million dollars worth of Italian sculpture and a gold-plated fish pond."

"But how could Harry time it so perfectly?"

"That's what the police would like to know. They figured some kind of triggering device, but they couldn't find it. And nobody could find Harry afterward."

"But why would he do such a thing?"

"According to the note he left me, it was because the man was a thief, a deposed political leader who'd looted his Caribbean island of money that the people badly needed. The publicity exposed him, and the money was returned."

"Good for Harry."

"There's just one minor problem. For a time it was touch and go with the State Department, until the details of the man's past came up. In the meantime they made an example of me. The publicity ruined me."

"But surely Harry cleared your name."

"Nope, he simply disappeared, leaving me to face the charges, pay the fines, and serve a little jail sentence when I couldn't. Eventually they released me, but the law's the law, and I was responsible for breaking it."

"But why did Harry leave?"

"I haven't a clue. The only thing I knew about Harry was his connection to Miss Rachel who lived in a Victorian mansion in Savannah. He made certain I knew about you."

And something made certain that I knew about you. Rachel didn't voice her belief, but it was there, and it was becoming stronger with every moment. Why, then, did that promised joy also bring such a strong sensation of fear?

"I'm very sorry about what happened to you, Cody. If I had any money, I'd give it to you. But I think you should know, I really don't know when or if Harry is coming back."

"Oh, he's coming back. He lured me here, and so far his plans seem to have all worked out as he intended. I think old Harry's like a pyromaniac. He starts a fire and stays around to watch it burn. He'll be back to watch me sweat."

Then Razor felt a sudden slash of cold at the back of his neck. He remembered the sounds of footsteps on the stairs, and the occasional sense of unease that came on little breaths of cold air. For one bizarre moment he wondered if Harry was already watching.

"Dammit, Rachel. You've got me thinking about ghosts and spirits. It's this house, all right, and the time of year. You know, it's almost Halloween. Fortune-tellers, black cats, ghosts—no wonder I'm feeling more spooky than Witchy walking on hot pavement."

"Yes, it's probably the time of year." But she knew it wasn't. For the tickley sensation was growing. Her knees felt weak, and her breathing seemed permanently impinged.

Razor wasn't sure he believed his own explanation, but what other rational solution was there? Razor put away the last dish and laid his drying cloth across the rack. He glanced around the kitchen, searching for a focus for his thoughts, a focus that didn't involve that bed beneath the eaves and the vision of Rachel in it. "Where do you mix up this special tea for Maude?"

"In here," she said, opening a door beside the fireplace and moving into the darkness. "I've turned this enclosed porch into my studio. Here are my teas. I order them from one of the reps who has an importing business on Factors Walk."

"Factors Walk?"

"The warehouse district down by the river,

where all the old merchants used to sell their China and Indian teas."

Razor followed Rachel inside, the pungent odor of all kinds of tea further assaulted his senses. He could smell, but he couldn't see a thing. "Where's the light switch?"

"Oops. Sorry. I sometimes forget. It's by the door."

Razor located and tried it. No luck. "Sorry, Rachel. It seems to have burned out, and I don't think I can replace overhead lights by candlelight."

At that moment the light came on, filling the room with a white glare. Rachel started, casting an odd look toward Razor. "Did something happen?" she asked.

"Something happened. The light just came on. Probably some kind of short in the wiring. Nothing unusual about that in these old places."

That explanation was reasonable, Razor thought, as he came to stand in the middle of the room with Rachel. As reasonable as the constant state of energy that seemed to follow the two of them. His body seemed to alternate between hot and cold. Now little licks of cold were hovering at the back of his neck again. And Witchy was sitting on the counter with her whiskers twitching and the suggestion of a smile on her lips.

"Cody . . . Cody, are we alone? I feel very

odd." Rachel reached out, taking his hand when it was offered and moving naturally into his embrace.

When the light went out moments later, Razor knew that his extrasensory perception was being assaulted. Wiring or coincidence he'd accept. Ghostly intervention he refused to acknowledge.

But he couldn't dismiss the feel of Rachel trembling in his arms. Nor could he stop himself from lowering his head, from operating on some kind of magnetic pull that drew his lips to hers. Anticipation burned hot as he found her mouth and felt it open beneath his touch as she melted against him.

Warm, dangerous feelings swirled around them, mixed with the smells and intensified into a force field of sensation. He couldn't see, and neither could she. Here, pressed together, they were equal and they were on fire, every movement matched one by the other, every pressure point touching its counterpoint in kind.

For that moment they were lost, held together by the physical presence of their desire. In the silence Witchy let out a sharp, satisfied cry and jumped to the floor. A tree limb scratched the glassed-in porch, and there was a heavy, creaking sound in the kitchen behind them.

Rachel knew that Cody was fighting what was happening. This wasn't what he wanted, yet he seemed powerless to stop kissing her. His hands, holding tightly to her bottom, flexed but didn't release their grip. Pressed against her was the evidence of his desire, pulsating as strongly as her own corresponding quiver of response.

Rachel knew they'd only been together for a matter of seconds, yet it seemed longer, and the need that flared between them was intensifying. This was destined to happen, but she hadn't expected it so quickly. She'd thought she was ready for this—but she wasn't, not yet.

Slowly she slid her hand between them and pressed against his chest, wrenching her lips away as she gasped for breath. "Cody."

He didn't release her instantly. Instead he continued to hold her, allowing his body to gear down, his hands to relax.

"I'm sorry," he growled, then caught sight of her confusion and forced himself to explain his concern. "Rachel, if you can really read my thoughts, you'd know inviting me to stay here wasn't smart."

"Sometimes I can. Sometimes my own emotions seem to block out yours."

The thought that she was as shaken up as he forced Razor to take a deep, calming breath. Finally he released her, except for holding her hand. "Did Harry leave that cat with you?"

"No. Witchy didn't appear until Harry had gone."

"I think *appear* is the proper word. If we could get that light to come back on, I think we'd find Witchy has vanished."

"She disappears frequently, last month for nearly a week. I thought she'd moved out, then one day she was back as if she'd never been gone." Rachel moved past him, leading him deftly through the darkness.

The overhead light didn't come on, but once they were back in the kitchen they discovered that Witchy *was* gone. And for the next few days Razor concluded that with the cat away, his emotional control had returned. There were no more creaking stairs and no cold breaths of air. But the return of that restraint didn't take away his desire for the woman who seemed unafraid of sharing her house with him.

He forced himself to take on every physical activity he could, convinced that if he worked hard enough he wouldn't feel the bizarre changes of temperature that rose and fell inside the house. For the last years he'd done little of the physical construction work of his firm. Now he was learning that he missed it.

Being tired might not take away his desire, but by working himself to a state of exhaustion he was able to conceal it. He replaced leaking, half-stopped-up pipes with new ones. He changed light bulbs. He rehung doors so that they opened and closed without sticking and replaced the bathroom tile. Finally Razor reached the point where he was ready to tackle the exterior filigree work around the Victorian cupola on the second floor.

"You don't have to do this, Cody," Rachel was saying as she swept the fallen leaves from the porch. "If you really want to do something, look at Maude's doorframe."

"Maude's doorframe isn't on my list, Rachel. If I do anything, it will be for you, to pay for my room and board."

"You're already buying more than half the food, so that isn't a fair exchange. Besides, Maude's been good to me, and I have no way to repay her. I would consider it a personal favor—to me."

In the end he couldn't refuse her. Later that afternoon he found himself walking with Rachel across the square and entering one of the more recently restored row houses on Abercorn Street. Where Rachel's house was sandwiched between two others, Maude's was joined to the dwelling on the other side, a kind of sister residence, common in the early days of Savannah's settlement.

"Thank you for coming, Cody," Maude said, holding a yapping Petey beneath her arm. "The doorframe is here, at the end of the foyer."

She touched a switch, bringing a myriad of light

into the room from a chandelier inside the hallway.

Razor let out a whistle of admiration at the wallpaper and carpeting and the lovely creamy color of the restored woodwork. "Nice. Whoever did this does good work."

"*Did* good work. The man was a true artist. He died last winter. Haven't found anyone who cared enough about what they are doing since. What do you think?"

Razor was studying the doorframe. *Doorframe* wasn't the term to apply to what he was seeing. There were two fluted pillars supporting a curved plastered arch between. One pillar had shifted and was sliding away from the section of wall it was holding up. The shift had cracked several chunks of plaster away from the ladyfinger design some artist had created with such detail.

"I think you'd better get some kind of brace up there before the entire section of plaster falls."

"Can you do it?" Maude asked.

"Probably, though I've never worked with anything like this."

"Will you do it?" This time the question came from Rachel, and it came at the moment he was formulating his refusal, came and changed his reply into a curt yes and a nod of agreement.

"Thank you," Maude said. "I'm more than willing to pay you a fair price. Goodness knows, you'll need money if you're going to satisfy the Historical Society on the repair of Rachel's house."

"Look, Maude, I'm not dealing with the Historical Society," he said in a voice that dared rebuttal. "I'm only here temporarily, and Rachel's house is a long-term project at best, possibly a project that isn't even practical."

"Don't pressure Cody, Maude. I've brought you a new tea sample. Shall I brew it while Cody is looking over the problem?"

"That would be nice," Maude agreed.

Cody watched as Rachel made her way past the tilting post and disappeared into the back of the house with Petey trotting happily along beside her.

"Good," Maude said, "I was wondering how I was going to talk to you alone."

"About what?"

"About Rachel of course. She's much too trusting, and I'm worried about your intentions."

I don't want even to think about my intentions, was what Razor wanted to say. *I have no intentions. Even if I can't keep from wanting her, I refuse to take advantage of her trust*. Instead he continued to examine the posts, letting Maude wait for her answer.

"I take it you don't intend to discuss your relationship with Rachel," Maude finally said.

"There isn't one, and if there were, I wouldn't discuss it."

"I see. Did she tell you about the city's stipulation about the time frame?"

"Time frame? No."

"When an unrestored house is bought in the Historic District, the owners must begin restoration within six months of the purchase, otherwise they must offer it for resale to the Historical Society."

"Generous with someone else's time, aren't they?"

"Rachel's house is a good example of why the ordinance was passed. Too many people bought houses with the idea of restoring them and didn't have either the money or the expertise. The houses continued to decay and finally reached a point where nobody even lived in them."

"Then it wasn't the Captain who kept residents away?"

Maude cocked her head in surprise. "You know about that old ghost story?"

"Of course. In fact I think I've had an encounter or two with the old boy."

"Rachel's never mentioned the pirate. I heard about him as a child, but I didn't know he was back. He's been gone for a long time."

"So I've been told. I'm waiting for him to appear in the flesh."

"Why? Are you some kind of psychic?"

"Not me. I don't even believe in that sort of

thing, and I already know more than I want to about Rachel's house." *And about Rachel.* "What I would like to know is more about this man who's into treasure hunting."

"Oh, you mean Jacques. Can't help you there. He came here a few weeks ago and met with the Historical Society. Claims to be a historian, doing research on ghosts and lost treasures. Is there a problem?"

"Not that I know of. But I think Rachel is a bit wary of him. Do you suppose you could ask a few questions? I mean, I'd feel better, once I'm gone, if there isn't some kind of nut running around."

"You're leaving? But I thought . . . I mean Rachel led me to believe that someone was coming to help her, and I thought it was you."

"So did she. Dammit, I just came her to find her uncle, not adopt her. I have enough trouble of my own. I can't take on someone else's."

"I see. Well, I wouldn't want to keep you if you're doing this against your will."

"I'm not. I mean, I am, but, hell, I said I would and I will. I'll rig a jack to support your wall while I decide how to repair the plaster."

"I can do that," Rachel said, reappearing in the hallway. "I mean I think I can if I can touch the original design. I once studied to be an artist, at least I started classes."

"Of course," Maude exclaimed. "I never thought about that. Cody, have you seen the little cat figures she sculpts from river clay?"

He hadn't. She'd mentioned them when they were in her studio. But the lights went out and he never noticed her efforts. There were so many sides to Rachel that he hadn't seen, and they all seemed designed to ensnare him in her life. He hadn't meant to agree to do more than make simple repairs on Rachel's house. He hadn't intended to take on Maude's problem. And he certainly didn't plan to stay around long enough to go into historical restoration. He kept telling himself that, but every time he opened his mouth, a yes seemed to come out when what he'd meant to say was no.

This time he couldn't blame his compliance on Witchy. She'd been gone for three days. He couldn't blame it on the Captain. The cold air had vanished with the cat. He couldn't blame it on Rachel, for she had stopped voicing her expectation that he was her knight on a white horse.

It was all the fault of those tarot cards, giving information that seemed to categorize their situation so neatly. He didn't need cards to tell what was behind him; he knew that. A lost business, a ruined reputation, and a lot of pain. He wasn't interested in what was ahead; he'd figure that out as it came. But he sure as hell needed an explanation for what happened every time he looked into Rachel's eyes and saw the trust there.

Trust.

Hope.

Acceptance.

Three things he'd long since lost. They'd gone with a father who had taken away a boy's childhood innocence and a mother who'd tried to replace it. And Harry, the crook who'd destroyed his dream.

Trust.

Acceptance.

Hope.

All those feelings emanated from Rachel, and she was forcing him to yearn for things he didn't want to believe in—ever again.

Then Witchy returned.

FOUR

"Do you really believe all that stuff with the cards?"

Razor and Rachel were finishing the painting of the repaired pillars and restored plaster in Maude's foyer. He'd thought he was past being a laborer, but working with Rachel was nice. Together they managed to reshape the chipped plaster and restore the beautiful old archway.

"I don't know. A boarding-school student brought back a deck from her summer vacation. I learned how to read them when I was sixteen. It was a way of drawing attention to myself while I was thumbing my nose at my teachers. I thought I was doing something that was sinfully wicked. The other girls smoked. I read the tarot cards."

"And did you have visions then?"

"No, not until after I was blind. Even now I don't see the answers in the cards. I can only say what the cards mean. Of course you mustn't tell any of my clients that. It would ruin my credibility."

Her admission of doubt should have reassured him. It didn't. He was still struggling with her belief that they would be lovers. She might claim that she wasn't sure about the cards, but he had the feeling that she was. There was almost an audible hum when they were together, and it was intensifying.

"I feel it, too, Razor," she said, as if he'd spoken aloud. "Don't think it's only you."

"It's this place, Rachel. You've created such a ghostly atmosphere that we carry it around with us."

"I'm sure you're right." But she wasn't. And it was becoming harder and harder to keep the kind of distance between them that Cody seemed to want.

"The plaster work is good, Rachel," he was saying. "You're very talented."

"So are you." Rachel was glad that the weather was growing a bit cooler, otherwise the heat they generated might become obvious to Maude. "Maude said you've accomplished what nobody else would even try, Cody. Why'd you stop?"

"Being a carpenter? Ambition. I wanted more than to do hourly labor. I wanted to have my own business, to be somebody—for my mother."

"You always talk about your mother. What about your father?"

"I don't even know where he is." Razor gave a

dry laugh. "He was always trying to be a big man. He liked showing off for the women. One day when I was a kid, he left with one of them."

"At least you still had your mother."

There was something stark about her voice. He glanced up to see her stilled brush, almost touching the surface but unmoving. Her eyes were open, but that uncertain look filled them with what he knew was deep pain. He had the uncomfortable feeling that she could see his memories as clearly as he did.

"What about your parents, Rachel? If you'd rather not talk about them, I'll understand. *I* don't—usually. The past is past, and what's gone I don't dwell on."

She gave him a quick, disbelieving look. "Except for Harry."

"Well, Harry's different. Harry's move was deliberate. And Harry isn't a part of me. I'm not even sure he's a part of you."

"He's the only family I've ever known. My mother brought me to the nuns when I was a baby, and I never saw her again. The nuns heard from her periodically. For a long time she even sent money. She always intended to come back and get me. Then, when I was twelve, she disappeared. By that time nobody wanted a painfully shy, budding teenager. But it wasn't so bad, not really. I never knew anything except being alone. I guess that's why I didn't panic when I lost my sight. And later Harry came."

Razor stretched his shoulders, partly to relax the tension, partly to relieve the soreness of his muscles. He didn't know what to say.

"How does our work look?" Rachel asked, trying to find her own way to defuse the tension that came in waves.

"Good, very good. And you're right. I'd forgotten the satisfaction that comes with doing the job yourself. It's been a long time."

Rachel dropped her brush into the bucket of cleaner and began wiping her hands with a moistened cloth. "I like working with my hands. I always have, it puts you in control."

"I'd forgotten that satisfaction. Twenty years ago, when I first started as a carpenter's helper, there was no satisfaction. What I did was because we needed money."

"It must have been hard working, going to school, and caring for your mother."

"Well, you got two out of three right. After my junior year there was no more school. My mother never knew that I dropped out to work full-time. She was too sick."

"I'm sorry. I loved school, especially college. It was a long struggle, but I can't imagine not being able to finish. Well, I guess I can. I was in my junior year of college when I met my mugger."

"Then why don't you finish? I did."

"You did?"

"Surprised?"

"No, not really. I think you're a very determined person, Cody. You can do anything you want."

"After my mother died, I went back at night and graduated from high school. Once I finished paying off her medical bills, I entered college. It took me eight years, but I finally got my degree."

He didn't have to tell her that he was a caring person, she'd known that. Now she was learning that he was a person who followed through. Her knight didn't abandon his family. "Your mother would have been very proud of your accomplishments, Cody."

"So was I, until Harry came along and destroyed them." He began gathering up their supplies and loading them in the truck.

"I don't think people around here would care what happened, Cody."

"Maybe not, if I wanted to be a carpenter the rest of my life. But that's not what I want, Rachel. I want my company back. I want my reputation restored. In the city of New Orleans right now I probably couldn't get a license to build a doghouse."

But Razor had already discovered that Rachel

was right about one thing. Because Rachel thought he could do no wrong, her neighbors didn't even ask about his past. He'd had enough offers from people who heard about Maude's doorframe to keep him busy for the winter. And he'd made a start on repairing the outside of Rachel's house, removing rotten wood, replacing cracked windowpanes, and getting the lower level ready for painting. If only he could stop the dreams, the dreams of Rachel in his arms. Working until it was time to sleep was the only way he kept his sanity.

Slowly it came to Razor that the last thing he wanted was to disappoint Rachel. She didn't talk much about what she'd said that first day. She wanted to believe what the tarot cards said about him because she needed to believe. But maybe she did have doubts. He sure as hell did. Still, at night, when the house was dark and the currents of air swirled around his loft room, he couldn't get past her startling revelations, beginning with the conviction that he would bring back her sight and ending, as it always did, with their being lovers.

Restoring her sight was easy to deal with. The idea was absurd. He was neither an ophthalmologist nor some kind of voodoo doctor. Though a few more nights of Rachel's dream visits and he might look one up.

Finally the supplies they were using in Maude's

repair job were stored and it was time to remove the beam he'd used as a brace. An inadvertent sigh escaped his lips.

"What's wrong, Cody, doesn't the paint look right?"

"No, it isn't that. The repair job is fine. No, not just fine, superior. I guess I'm a little tired."

"You haven't been sleeping well, have you?"

"You should know."

He backed carefully down the foyer and started out the door with the beam.

"Why did you say I should know? I don't understand." Rachel followed the sound of his voice and stepped out on the porch, catching the banister as she waited for his reply.

"Rachel, I don't understand this gift you have, this special sight, but it's driving me crazy. I can't tell whether I'm dreaming or you're really in my room at night."

"Which do you want it to be?"

"I don't know. But I swear I've seen you, as clearly as I see you right now. You're always wearing some kind of flimsy robe, and you're not wearing anything underneath."

Rachel gave a relieved laugh. He hadn't actually seen her. "Cody, I wear a granny gown. There's nothing flimsy about it. I think you're suffering from some kind of erotic fantasy. What do I do when I come to your room?"

Distracted by the instant picture of Rachel standing in his doorway, he dropped the beam in the back of his truck with more force than he'd intended. "Nothing, and that's what's driving me up the wall. You get close enough for me to want—I mean you come to the bed and then you leave."

Rachel smiled. He *was* distraught. She'd felt the increased tension between them since he'd kissed her, and she'd tried to reduce it by staying away when they weren't working. Because it disturbed him, she'd stopped talking about why he was there, or his staying.

There'd been no more innocent touching, and he had made no attempt to kiss her again. Keeping her distance had been hard. The excitement, the anticipation was new to her, as was the way her pulse would race unexpectedly and her body would flare hot with starbursts of sensation under her skin. Her reaction to Cody was so much more than she'd anticipated, and she was as out of kilter as Cody seemed to be.

Yet his having dreams about her coming to him was something she hadn't foreseen. Nothing had taken her beyond his arrival. He would come to her and she'd see again. The startling conviction that they'd be lovers hadn't come until she'd read his cards. That puzzled her.

For days she'd searched for a reason. Always before, answers had come to her unasked and unbidden, in little scenes, like vignettes on the mind's screen. But this time she was lost. She was beginning to wonder if she'd been wrong about the interpretation of her visions. She wanted, no, needed to know more.

"You say I'm inside your room. When I come to you, you don't want me to leave?"

"No! Well, yes. Hell, this is weird enough without complicating things, Rachel. You don't want to know what I want. Get in the truck!"

What he wanted was what he wanted every time he looked at her, to take her to his bed and lose himself in the maelstrom of emotion that swirled constantly around them. To touch and taste and be a part of the reality of her.

Rachel smiled at his short-tempered reply.

"And stop reading my thoughts. This isn't some psychic vision you're dealing with here. This is a man who's stuck in a house that's falling down around him, with a trusting woman who ought to be running as hard as she can in the opposite direction."

"I'm not running, Cody."

"I know. It's all some kind of giant conspiracy

Harry's set up to keep me here—for what I don't know."

"And is it working?"

"Hell, yes!"

Rachel got in the truck, barely closing the door before Razor roared off, a squeal of his tires breaking the afternoon silence. He felt as if he were being manipulated. He knew it and he didn't seem to be able to do a thing about it. Drawing on the anger he felt for Harry, he closed out the woman hanging on to the door as he turned corners and bounced over curbs.

He was making no headway in finding Harry. Instead he was becoming more involved in Rachel's life. That had to stop. There must be a way of locating that crook. He couldn't have simply vanished into thin air. He bought this house; somebody had to have information on him. Maybe waiting wasn't the answer. Becoming responsible for Miss Rachel Kimble sure wasn't what he had in mind.

"I'm sorry, Cody. I don't know what else to say, except you're free to go at any time. You really don't have to worry about me."

"Sure. And what will you do?"

"I'll manage."

"You'll manage? How? I don't even know how *I'll* manage. You don't have a job, neither do I. You have no money. Neither do I, at least not enough to start up a company."

"But you just earned two hundred dollars' profit, and if Maude had had her way, it would have been more."

"Rachel, I do not intend to be some neighborhood handyman. I was only helping your friend because you asked me to."

"Oh? And what's that stuff you stacked on my back porch?"

"A few supplies I need to repair the front steps and—damn!" He broke off, hit the brakes, and made a sharp turn into the lane behind Rachel's house. He was doing it again, planning a future he had no intention of carrying out. "What made the city decide to make all these streets one-way, anyhow?"

Rachel bit back a laugh. Cody was having a difficult time being a nice guy. Maybe he was right. Maybe a good night's sleep was in order, for both of them. She'd make him a nice cup of her special blend of relaxing tea.

Razor caught sight of the smile on Rachel's lips. There was something unnerving about a woman knowing what he was thinking, even if she couldn't see his glowering expression. "Get out, Rachel. I have an errand to run."

"Oh? Where are you going?"

"To see about having a telephone installed. If I'm going to find Harry, I'm going to need some help."

"You're going to hire someone to look for Harry?"

"That's exactly what I'm going to do."

"Can you afford—"

"Certainly, Miss Rachel Kimble. I just made two hundred dollars for three days' work. I'm a rich man!"

"I'll get supper," she said, and slid out of the truck.

"Don't bother. I'm only a boarder, remember. Don't wait up. I don't know when I'll be back. And stash that yellow-eyed cat somewhere. I'm tired of her watching me."

Rachel dashed through the house and stood on the front porch as Cody rounded the corner and drove past. She'd already learned to recognize the sound of his truck. But she was puzzled. Another vehicle was coming to a stop behind Cody. There was an odd rattle of two pieces of metal clattering against each other. For a moment she thought she'd heard that same clatter before.

Then both vehicles were gone, and Rachel felt an odd sense of foreboding. Cody had been in her house for almost a week now. Underneath the aura of emotion that surrounded them while they'd worked together, she'd experienced a sense of contentment that apparently hadn't spread to her boarder. He seemed short-tempered and unwilling to accept her contention that he was supposed to be here. It was becoming obvious that she'd been fooling herself. She might be happy with Razor around, but he wasn't.

That's why he was going off to hire someone to look for Harry. The sooner Harry was found, the sooner Cody could get out of her life.

Why on earth had she ever thought that they could be a team? She turned and started up the steps to the porch. If she'd had any tears left, she would have shed one. Opening the door, she was greeted first by Witchy and then by the smell of a pipe.

A pipe? She knew only one person who smoked a pipe.

"Harry? Is that you, Harry?"

"Of course, darling. Who else are you expecting? Come and give me a hug?"

"Where are you?"

She'd never understood why she could sense things about everyone except Harry. His arms tightened around her, and she recognized that special crisp sea-breeze smell of his cologne and the scratchy feel of his whiskers on her cheek.

"Oh, Harry, where have you been? There's so much I have to tell you."

"Not now, love. I just dropped in to get your signature on these papers. Come over here."

He let her go and tucked a pen into the curve of her hand. "Let's move to the table. I've laid a ruler along the line where you're to sign."

"What am I signing?"

"I'm transferring another piece of property into your name, a building on the river. I'm mortgaging it in the transfer, temporarily of course. I have a friend who is in a bit of trouble and I need the money."

"But, Harry. I don't think I can make a second house payment. I mean, I'm barely managing. Even with my ceramics, my tea, and my readings, I haven't even made the October payment on this house, and the Historical Society—"

"Don't worry, love. I'll take care of it. One day soon you'll have more money than you'll ever need. Trust me!"

"I do trust you, Harry. But that isn't all. Cody's here."

"Really? Good. I knew he'd find you."

All the while Harry was guiding Rachel toward the table, until the seat of the chair was pressing against the back of her knees.

"It's you he's looking for, Harry. You do know that he's angry with you."

"Ah, yes. I thought he might be. But that will change soon enough. Sign right here, darling."

And Rachel found herself complying. After all, Harry had done so much for her. He'd come for her when she'd been alone with nowhere to go. It was he who had bought her little house. If he needed funds, she couldn't refuse.

"Harry, Cody seems quite determined."

"I know, darling. I wouldn't have picked a man for you who wasn't."

"Picked a man for me? I don't understand."

"You will. Very soon."

Harry was leaving. She knew it, and that knowledge surprised her. Until now she'd had no feelings, no visions, no special awareness connected with Harry. Just the conviction that he cared about her.

Had she been so desperate that she'd allowed her judgment to be impaired? Maybe she'd been wrong.

"Don't doubt yourself, Rachel. I picked Razor Cody because I knew you'd like him. He's as ornery as I am and just as stubborn. He'll be with you when I'm long gone, love. You'll be glorious together."

"I'm not sure anymore, Harry. And I'd better warn you. He plans to shave your head, cut it off, and leave."

Harry chuckled. "Definitely a man after my own heart, or in this case, my head. All you have to do now is keep him, *any way you can*. Find a way to do that, Rachel. And darling, don't tell him I was here."

"But, Harry, I don't understand."

"You will, darling. You will."

And just as suddenly as he'd come, he was gone, leaving Rachel with his promise that she and Cody would be "glorious together."

Still steaming, Razor made the telephone company his first stop. He sailed past a parking place, then watched in disbelief as the driver in the green van behind him actually backed up and allowed Razor to pull in.

As Razor walked into the office, he kept an eye on the van that was still idling in the drive, as if he were waiting for someone to come out. Nobody did. He shook off his unease. It was all Rachel's fault. He couldn't shake his mysterious thoughts when he was with her, or when he was alone. She seemed permanently etched in his mind.

Or, if he were honest, the etchings he was fighting were duplicated a little lower. He seemed permanently hard, and his body ached from denial.

Inside the telephone company the service representative took his deposit and made the arrangements to have the phone installed. The lady behind the counter directed Razor to the Historical Society's Planning Commission, who ran him through the wringer about their regulations, then referred him to City Hall. The property clerk confirmed that the deed to the house was in Rachel Kimble's name and referred him to the mortgage holder. There Razor learned the final truth.

Only a minimum down payment had been made on the Victorian row house, using another piece of property on the docks as collateral. On closer examination he found the newly executed mortgage on the second piece of property that had just been transferred into Rachel's name.

Razor was reasonably certain that Rachel didn't know she owned two houses. And they were both mortgaged to the hilt, with payments due on the first of each month. More strings to hold him. For he not only wanted her body now, he wanted to make her life easier.

Razor stuffed his hands in his pockets and walked across the rocky pathway made from ballast stones of the sailing ships of long ago. He headed down to the water's edge. To the right was Factors Walk, a series of warehouses now converted into bars, restaurants, and quaint little shops. But it was to the left where the numbers placed Rachel's second piece of property.

Curiously, Razor studied the buildings. He found himself squaring his shoulders uncomfortably. There was something peculiar about the vacant street. There was nobody walking along the river except him, yet he felt as if he were being watched. And this time it wasn't the cat.

He passed boarded-up building after building, unused and falling down. Until he came to the number he'd copied from the papers. The building in question couldn't be worth much. Razor didn't understand what Harry had wanted with it, nor why he'd put it in Rachel's name.

The door was locked, the side windows boarded up. Only the grimy front window was uncovered. Shading his eyes, Razor peered inside. He couldn't see anything and doubted that there was anything to see. Finally he turned away. He'd come back in the daytime and check out the structure.

What he wanted now was to be alone, to think about this obsession he had for Rachel. He picked a bar and went in. At six o'clock the happy hour was past happy and into early maudlin. At the piano a thin woman was singing a river song about lost love and broken promises.

Razor ordered a long-neck beer and nursed it while he considered his situation. From New Orleans he'd driven to Savannah, ready to jerk a knot in the man who'd caused him so much grief.

Instead he'd met Rachel, who had drawn him into her life as if she'd measured him, created a mold around the two of them, and poured him into it.

Without knowing how it had happened, he'd suddenly found himself convincing the restoration board that he was the carpenter who would be handling the refurbishing of Rachel's house. He'd committed himself to something he had no intention of doing. Yet he'd already made a start; they could see that. It hadn't been easy, but because they liked Rachel, they'd decided to give her time.

Razor took a long swallow of the flat beer and ran his hands through his hair. There was something about Savannah. He decided it made him think of his mother and the things Razor hadn't been able to do when he was seventeen. He felt as if he'd stumbled into some kind of time warp, a modern-day Brigadoon, a fantasy from which he couldn't seem to find a way out. Rachel needed him, and this time he had a chance to make things right.

Two hours later, convinced that his guilt over his father's abandonment led to a sense of responsibility for Rachel, Razor headed back to his truck. His desire was understandable; he'd been in jail. He'd simply been too long without a woman. Away from Rachel's overpowering presence, he'd solved the problem.

The van that had deferred to Razor's truck was

now parked in the adjoining space. Razor studied it for a moment, then cranked the engine and drove slowly back toward Rachel's house. This was one night he was grateful for one-way streets and lack of traffic in the neighborhood. After running into two parks that turned him away, he finally found the proper lane and pulled in.

Lane! Hell, in New Orleans this would be an alley. It would smell bad, be dirty, and be too tight for driving, but it would be honest and call itself what it was, an alley.

At this time of day back in New Orleans he'd be heading for his apartment and a good night's sleep. But he wasn't in New Orleans and he'd been fooling himself about his desire for the woman inside. He'd eventually sleep tonight, but he'd dream about Rachel.

The house was dark. Razor didn't know whether that meant Rachel was in bed or she'd simply forgotten to turn on the lights. He went from room to room, flipping switches until the pitiful house was blazing with light, then went upstairs. Rachel's bedroom was empty. She was gone. Even the damned cat was gone.

Razor started up the stairs to his third-floor room, and sank down wearily on the steps. Where was she? He felt a coldness about him that wasn't like the little licks that he blamed on their ghost captain's presence. This was an emptiness, the way his childhood home had felt after his mother was gone.

He didn't like it.

For a man with the reputation of being a loner, he didn't like being alone. He never had.

FIVE

Razor was still sitting on the stairs when he heard them come in, Rachel and a man. He didn't know the voice, but other than Mr. Grossman and another elderly neighbor, Rachel's male friends hadn't crossed his path.

"This was nice, Rachel, very nice. Would you allow me to take you out to dinner tomorrow night? Perhaps to the Pirate House?"

"I don't think so, Jerry, but thank you for asking. Would you like a cup of tea?"

"That would be nice."

Nice? The stranger's voice was neither firm nor hesitant, just hopeful. Of course it would be nice to come in and have a cup of tea with Rachel. Razor grimaced as he listened, his stomach feeling as if it were trying to crawl up into his lungs.

The floor creaked slightly as Rachel's guest followed her down the hallway. He was not too heavy, not too light. Like the littlest bear in the fairy tale, the man with Rachel sounded just right.

But he wasn't. Razor felt as if he'd suddenly been endowed with some of Rachel's second sight. He found himself coming to his feet and moving as silently as possible down the stairs.

You're feeling like that knight on a white horse, he told himself, ready to protect her. *That's natural.* But his stomach muscles were squeezing themselves into tight little knots, and he knew that what he was feeling was more.

The murmur of voices was too low for him to understand, and occasionally he heard Rachel laugh. It was the laughter, uneasy laughter, that bothered him, bothered the hell out of him. Who was this joker? Rachel hadn't said anything earlier about going out. Of course he'd been gone all afternoon, and what she did was her business. He certainly hadn't told her what he'd planned to do.

Suddenly Witchy appeared at the foot of the stairs, eyeing him with obvious agitation. She ran up the steps, then back down again as if she were trying to tell him something. Something urgent.

Razor walked into the foyer. She turned and danced away, purring in that short, anxious little way she had of letting him know what she wanted.

Obviously Witchy wasn't pleased with Rachel's guest either.

There was silence in the kitchen as Razor entered, silence but not inactivity, for Rachel was struggling with the man she'd come home with. He was attempting to kiss her, holding her arms and pressing her against the sink as she moved her head back and forth.

"Oh, sorry. I didn't know you were back, Rachel." Razor watched the man fall back. "Hello, I'm Razor Cody. I don't believe we've met."

"Cody, you're home." Rachel came to Razor's side. "I'm sorry you didn't get back in time to attend the concert in the park. I ran into Jerry there, and he was kind enough to see me home."

"Thank you, Jerry. That was very nice of you." Razor's words were evenly spaced, proper in every respect. But there was no doubt about the icy threat in his tone.

"I didn't realize you had someone here, Rachel," Jerry said.

"She does."

"Rachel?" Jerry turned toward her, uncertain whether or not to believe Razor.

"Yes, Jerry, Cody is staying here with me."

"I see." Jerry took another look at Razor and moved quickly around him. "Good night, Rachel.

I'm sorry if I was out of line. I'll see you—another time."

The door slammed.

Rachel stood in the silence. She didn't know what to say. She'd waited all afternoon for him to return, her nerves drawn to a frazzle. When he hadn't, she'd finally left the house, intending to walk off her tension. There was a concert in the park. She'd stopped to listen, trying to fill the painful void she'd felt over Cody's absence.

Then Jerry had come, serving as a distraction, and she'd allowed him to walk her home. She hadn't expected him to try to kiss her. Now she felt as if she'd done something very wrong.

Razor, watching her chew anxiously on her lower lip, found himself at a loss for words. His head was aching from having had too much to drink and his breath was tight from the sudden picture of Rachel being helpless against the man's advances. They were like two circling animals, both wary of the other's intent, but neither able to dominate.

Finally Rachel spoke. "Thank you, Cody, but you didn't need to worry about me. Jerry is a bit of a pest, but I've always managed to handle him."

"Like you were handling him when I came in?"

But was she really trying to handle him tonight? She didn't know. She'd known that Cody was at home. She'd sensed his presence and felt relief, followed swiftly by anger that he'd walked away without talking about their problem. Jerry had been kind, and she'd needed the reassurance of someone who was a part of her everyday world.

She hadn't asked Cody to come into her life and, no matter what the cards said, she wasn't asking anything of him now. Yet she knew a deep pang of regret. For asking and wanting were two different things. And she felt shame that she'd encouraged Jerry because she'd hoped Cody was watching.

For most of her life she'd struggled to take care of herself. This afternoon, after Cody had driven away, she'd tried to look at her situation logically. She didn't need anybody. She'd been an unwanted child, and that had hurt. She'd taken that pain and made it work for her, turning her life into a series of small successes. There'd been no time for men, nor any trust either. Until Harry had come. Then Cody. And she couldn't be sure whether her easy acceptance was because of her gift or a need that she'd refused to acknowledge—until now.

What she was forced to admit was she'd given Jerry her unspoken approval to kiss her, not because she wanted Jerry. She'd been convincing herself that she didn't need Cody and punishing him because he'd made her know what it felt like to want a man who turned away from that need. He made her ashamed.

She'd wanted Cody to see Jerry. She'd wanted to make him jealous, angry, angry enough to forget the safe distance they'd kept between them. But now she didn't know what to do, except feel guilty for her childishness.

"You're right, Cody. I—I wanted to punish you."

His voice was barely more than a groan. "Why?"

"Because I wanted you to want to kiss me, to tell me that it was all right for me to want you, and you didn't."

Witchy meowed.

Razor felt the nerve at the corner of his eye twitch. His mouth was dry and his breathing harsh. All right for her to want him? She thought he didn't want her. He'd tried to convince himself of the same thing. They were both wrong. There was nothing he wanted more. He wanted to kiss her and pull those long skirts and flowing blouses from her body, to find the woman beneath who called out to him in his dreams. Here he was standing in her kitchen as hard as he'd ever been in his life and he felt like a damned fool.

Like Don Quixote tilting at windmills. Like Lancelot coming to the defense of Guinevere. Like Han Solo lusting after the Princess. Like the knight on a white horse she'd accused him of being. He was losing his resolve. It was time for him to get out of this house, before he did something really dumb, like give in to his desire.

Rachel felt the tension and forced herself to relax slightly. Demanding a reaction from him was wrong. She'd never been considered devious, she'd never resorted to cheap tricks. She couldn't now. "Cody, I'm sorry. It was wrong of me to do this."

"You're right, Rachel. I'm a man who travels alone. I do whatever I do with the full knowledge of the end result, and I'm ready to take the consequences of my action. In other words I believe in an eye for an eye and a tooth for a tooth."

"I'm sorry you've been hurt," she said softly, straightening her back.

Lord, how long had it been since someone had apologized to him? Cared about him? A long time. But it hadn't mattered before. He hadn't needed comfort or forgiveness. He wasn't used to it, and he didn't know how to handle it. He'd been satisfied with his life until he'd arrived in Savannah and Rachel had willingly made him a part of her world.

He hadn't intended to enjoy it, hadn't intended to find a place for himself in it, had never considered the outcome. When had this need started to matter?

She was looking at him as if she could see, as if every emotion he was feeling was rippling across his face in hot neon.

The cat meowed again.

"Come, Witchy," Rachel said suddenly with the hint of a catch in her voice, "it's time for us to go to bed. We have a busy day tomorrow."

She started to move past Cody, the scent of her tantalizing him with her nearness, the hem of her skirt brushing his leg.

He caught her arm to stop her. He couldn't let her go. "What are you doing tomorrow?"

"I have to pick up a new shipment of tea and deliver my latest order of ceramic cats to Maude's shop. Why?"

"If you want to go out to dinner, I'll take you."

"That would be nice, Cody."

Nice! There it was again, that word *nice*. Except right now he didn't feel very nice. He felt angry. He felt as if he were flying apart, spinning like one of those children's tops where the rings of color blended into one blur as it whirled about the floor.

"Who else drinks your blackberry tea, Rachel?" he asked.

He knew before she spoke what her answer would be. He knew, and cringed, when she softly said, "Jerry."

The night air seemed more charged than usual as Razor tried to force his keyed-up body to wind down enough to fall asleep. But it was no use. He couldn't be still. Lying there in the darkness, wearing only his briefs, his nerve endings seemed charged with kinetic energy. He rubbed the back of his neck.

Calluses on his hands pricked at the skin beneath his hair. Too long, he decided. He needed a haircut. If he were going to satisfy the city fathers and find a way to make enough money to do the work on Rachel's house before he moved on, he needed to look trustworthy.

He was doing it again, making plans for Rachel's house.

He needed . . . damn! He needed a woman. He needed Rachel Kimble.

With an oath of disgust he came to his feet and padded to the window. There was a full moon outside, a fat Harvest Moon, filling the district with light almost as bright as day. The house faced the river, giving him a bird's-eye view of the barges moving through the darkness, lights flickering through the bare tree limbs. He could see the neatly lined streets, dating back to the original design for the city by the settlers.

According to the brief history lesson the historians had given him this afternoon, the mulberry trees, brought to the colonies to start a silk business, had long since died. In fact the Trustees' Garden, in which all the experimental plants and trees had been planted, had been abandoned. The only remaining part was on the grounds of one of the city's most famous restaurants, the Pirate House.

That was where Jerry had suggested they have dinner. Razor cursed again. If anybody took Rachel to dinner, it would be him. They'd go to the Pirate House.

Pirate.

Captain Perine.

That was all it took to conjure up the sound of footsteps on the stairs leading to his room. But this time the steps didn't falter, they came to the door and inside, into the moonlight streaming through the window.

It was Rachel, standing there as she had every night since he'd arrived. Except tonight he wasn't asleep. Tonight he wasn't even in bed. And tonight she wasn't wearing the filmy robe, nor the granny gown. Her pale-blond hair was falling across bare shoulders, turning to gold in the light.

"Rachel," he whispered hoarsely. "You don't want to do this."

"Yes, Cody. I do. I surely do."

She'd known he had the proud spirit of a lion. The lion was the king of the jungle, powerful, his dark essence in tight control. Rachel could feel that control thrumming through the night.

She could feel his need, too, and as she curled against him, he seemed to jerk away for a moment, then all resistance flew out of his body and he pulled her into his powerful arms.

"Are you sure, Rachel?" His voice was husky with emotion.

She brushed her mouth across his chin and whispered two words, "I'm sure."

Razor knew he was lost. God knew he'd tried to stay away. Their kisses had been enough to forecast how they'd be together, and he'd honestly tried to back away. He knew, even as he felt her body against him, that he was making a mistake, but he couldn't stop himself.

Razor's hands trembled as he touched her beautiful face, committing to memory that which he could see and she could only imagine. And then their lips met.

As if she were the one with sight and he were blind, she opened herself up to his touch. There were words, but neither knew who spoke, nor what was said. For this was not a time for promises or whispered words of commitment. This was a time for speaking with their bodies and committing themselves with a caress.

"I think I have waited for you always, Cody."

"I don't understand why, but I believe that."

She slid her hand down his chest, across his

belly, and lower, reaching his briefs and shyly touching his arousal. "You're not wearing clothes, Cody."

He tried not to tremble beneath her curious touch. "Neither are you, Miss Rachel. Why is that?"

"I want nothing between us, nothing held back."

"So be it."

"You are, I think, a very special man." She touched his eyebrows, his nose, moving her fingers across his strong chin, down the corded muscles of his neck, down his chest until she came to his nipple, where she stopped and tilted her head in question.

"There is something here?"

A ripple ran down his spine at the depth of her insight. "Yes, a tattoo."

"Why?"

"I don't know now. At the time I suppose I thought it was macho. I'd been out drinking with my crew, celebrating being made job foreman." He caught her fingertips and drew them to his lips. "It was dumb."

"No, it's part of you. What is it?"

"It's a knife, a dagger."

She leaned down and brushed his nipple with her lips. "Is that where you got your name?"

"No, I picked that up in the marines. From the straight razor I used."

She couldn't keep herself from asking, "To kill?"

"No, to shave." But both of them knew that was a lie built of kindness. He might not have used his razor to kill, but he would have if it had been necessary.

Rachel shivered.

"Do I frighten you, Rachel?"

"Nothing about you frightens me, Cody, except the way you make me feel."

He lifted her and carried her to his small bed, laying her down and standing back so that he could see her. "And how do I make you feel?"

"As though I'm losing myself. As if this Rachel Kimble is disappearing forever. I seem to keep reinventing myself. There was my life before I lost my eyes and my life since. Now there is my life with you."

Razor came down on the bed beside her, lying on his side, resting on one elbow. Like Rachel he was caught up in a need to touch, to know, to claim the body of this perfect woman who'd come to him. Once more he found her lips and felt her open herself to him, following his lead, learning quickly to respond to questions he asked with his touch.

Awash now in hot sensation, she blossomed beneath his touch, opened herself up to him until their tangled bodies signaled the urgent need for more, until he moved over her, feeling her agitated movements beneath him, until he found the place that welcomed him with unexpected heat. Then, after the hesitation of encountering a momentary obstruction, they were joined, and Razor might have been twenty-one again and caught up in the celebration of his triumph. Rachel became the artist who tattooed his skin with her essence, who was crowned by the majesty of their release.

Later, as the moon slid behind the trees and hid its light behind nature's leaf-shorn fans, Razor lay watching her sleep. What had happened had been profound.

He'd seen Rachel in this bed every night since he'd arrived. Now she was really there, in his arms, in his most secret heart. He didn't want to think about the significance of that thought, about the lingering satisfaction, about the vulnerability of the man who'd made love to a woman who'd seen him coming and accepted him when he'd arrived.

For now, basking in the peaceful afterglow was enough. She'd seen them as lovers, and that prediction had come true. She'd told him about his future, about his company, about this night. They'd also spoken of violent passion and misunderstanding, success and love. Still to come was her conviction that he'd restore her sight. She was committed to her belief. Suppose she was wrong? What would happen to Rachel? What would happen to them?

The next time he woke, she was gone. Only her scent lingered in the tangled sheets. For a long time he simply lay trying to gather his thoughts. Then, with an uncharacteristic lightheartedness, he sprang to his feet, pulled on a pair of jeans, and bounded down the steps to find coffee warming on the stove and Witchy napping on the windowseat.

"Meow?" she said, and came lazily to her feet, daintily licking her foot and washing her face.

"Where is she?"

The cat didn't answer. Razor poured himself a cup of coffee and continued the conversation as if he expected the cat to respond.

"Where were you last night, cat? I know you know that we—that Rachel and I—that—" He hesitated, then continued, talking to himself as much as to the cat.

"We made love, cat. We spent the night in each other's arms, and it wasn't a fantasy. It was real, cat. Real!"

"Meow" was Witchy's vague reply as she flounced down from her seat and strolled leisurely off up the stairs.

The cat was getting fat. Razor crossed his arms around his waist and tested the area under his ribs.

So was he, or he soon would be if he didn't get back to work.

"Rachel?"

But there was no answer this time. Even the cat had abandoned him.

"Good morning, Miss Kimble," Jacques Devoe said, coming alongside of Rachel as she left Jerry's Tea Company, where she'd replenished her supplies. "I understand that you're making good progress on your house. I didn't know that your carpenter was living with you."

"Cody is staying there, yes." She couldn't keep a smile from curling her lips. He was there, waiting for her. She'd move his things down to her room now. There'd be no going back to separate beds.

"Cody, huh. I take it that he's a bit more than just a hired hand?"

Rachel felt a current of something disturbing chase away her happiness. She hastened her step and said lightly, "Why would you think that?"

"You're positively radiant. Maybe it will enhance your psychic powers. I've heard that the higher the emotional state, the more likely you are to receive a message."

"Mr. Devoe, I've tried to explain to you that I don't receive visions. I only read the tarot cards.

Perhaps you might want to consult someone who has psychic powers."

"Oh, no. You're the one I want. I'm very sure of that. But I'll not intrude any longer for now. Good morning, Miss Kimble."

Rachel heard him move away with relief. Her association with Jacques Devoe was becoming uncomfortable, and she wasn't sure why. He seemed to expect more of her than she was prepared to give. And though she didn't tell him, she was sensing a disturbing emotional chasm that she didn't understand. At their next session she'd tell him that she couldn't help him anymore.

Shaking off the sense of gloom that had fallen over her, Rachel pushed her cart into Maude's shop. "Hello?"

There was nothing subtle about Maude's "What's wrong?"

"Nothing, absolutely nothing. The world is absolutely beautiful this morning."

Maude chortled. "You've slept with him, haven't you?"

Rachel considered putting her off with a shocked disavowal, then realized that simply thinking about Cody had brought back all those wonderful feelings they'd shared the night before. Rachel felt too good to hide the truth. "Yes," she said simply. "Am I awful?"

"I think you're lucky. Isn't he the most dangerous-looking man you've ever seen? Oops, bad choice of words."

"But of course you're right. I've never really seen him. But he isn't dangerous. He's powerful. He's determined. He knows his own mind and he gives as good as he gets."

"Uh-huh, and from the looks of you, I'd say you enjoyed every good he gave out. Is he going to make an honest woman out of you?"

Rachel started. She hadn't dared allow herself to think farther than the moment. Tomorrow was still that dark tunnel with no light at the end. "If you mean marriage, I don't know. I never thought about it, but I don't think Cody is the kind of man who is into marriage and permanence."

"Too bad, but that's the way with the special ones," Maude said with resignation.

"He is special, isn't he?"

Maude agreed, adding, "I trust you're thinking about caution, Rachel. I mean, I know you're an innocent, and passion is wonderful, but there are things such as disease and pregnancy."

"Babies?" She couldn't keep the pleasure from her voice. For years she'd refused to allow herself to think about marriage and a family. She'd struggled to live and go to school. Anything else was out there, in the future. Then came the accident, and survival had been the foremost thing on her mind.

Not a family. Not babies. Not being married to Cody.

"Yes, those things that happen when you aren't prepared. You are prepared, aren't you, Rachel?"

"Do you mean am I using some kind of birth control? No, there was never a need. Oh, Maude, do you suppose that it's possible that I could have a baby? I love children. I always have."

"It's possible. In fact it's even probable if you don't get yourself to the doctor. I'll call and make an appointment for you with my doctor. In the meantime don't let the man near you without protection. Do you understand what I'm saying?"

Protection? Sure, she knew about condoms. You couldn't listen to the television or the radio without hearing about the need to practice safe sex. She knew about them, but she had no knowledge of using them. There were so many things that her special gift didn't reveal.

Maude wrote Rachel a check for her portion of the sales of the little cat figures, gave her a hug, and closed the door with a jingle of its bell.

Rachel, lost in memories of her time with her knight on a white horse, was at the curb before she knew where she was. She had to wait for the surge of footsteps around her before she crossed East Bay

Street and headed down Habersham toward her house. Last night Cody had promised to take her to the Pirate House for dinner, and she wanted to have the day to plan what she'd wear.

The air was heavy this morning. The radio was beginning to voice warnings about a tropical storm meandering about the Atlantic. It would miss the islands, but whether it would turn toward the Gulf or move up the coast was yet to be determined.

By the time Rachel reached her house, she could hear someone moving down the steps and back up again. She waited until her ears told her that she was the only one there, then made her way inside her little house. The front door was open. There was a smell of wood and the sound of a drill.

"Excuse me?" Rachel said, and waited for someone to speak.

"Rachel, come in," Cody said with an odd tone in his voice. "They're installing the phone. I had them put in an outlet in the kitchen and one in the bedroom. I hope that meets with your approval."

"Everything about you meets with my approval. What else do you have planned for this morning?"

A hand reached out and grabbed her, pulling her into an embrace. "This." He kissed her, and she knew that was why she'd hurried back to her house.

"Are you always so delicious, Mr. Cody?"

"That, and innovative and thorough and passionate—and very hungry."

"I'll fix you some breakfast."

"You are my breakfast."

"I hope so, Cody. But I think you might need more than kisses to keep your strength up."

"That isn't what's up, and work certainly isn't what I've been thinking about all morning."

Cody told himself that he was a simple man, a construction worker, not some deep thinker. His work was physical and demanding, and he made his own decisions. But this morning he was running on autopilot, and if he was heading for self-destruct, it was full speed ahead.

Witchy meandered through, found her food bowl, and sat down, discussing its empty status with increasing velocity.

"I think your cat is hungry," Razor said. "I also think she's getting fat."

"Good for her. That shows she's content. A woman ought to be content, Cody. I highly recommend it."

He kissed Rachel again and held her tight, feeling the aura of their closeness spill into the room.

"They're installing the phone upstairs now," he said as he glanced at the tea in her cart, thought of Jerry, then pushed that unexpected jealous thought out of his mind.

"That's good, I suppose. At least now my clients can call for an appointment for a reading."

Another jealous thought. He didn't want anybody coming for a reading, even if that was part of Rachel's income. He didn't like the idea of strangers coming into her house, strangers she couldn't see. Before he left, he'd get her a dog. That would be some protection anyway.

"The mailman came," he said. "Brought you two letters from the bank, one from the Historical Society, and a bill from the power company. Maude called and said she's arranged for your doctor's appointment. Are you ill?"

"No." She blushed as she remembered her conversation with Maude.

"Then why are you going to the doctor?"

"It's for—I mean you and I—we—"

He understood her hesitation. "You're going to the doctor because of me. Because we—you're going on the pill?"

"Yes. I never expected to need it. But I think I'd better. Maude thinks it would be a mistake for me to get pregnant—to have a baby."

Rachel having a baby. Rachel heavy with a child, his child. The thought took the breath out of Razor Cody, that and the memory of his father walking out the door.

"Maude is a lot smarter than I gave her credit

for," he snapped, took one look at the joy fading from her face, and wished he hadn't spoken. "I mean, you could get pregnant, if you aren't already."

Christ, why hadn't he considered the possibility? It hadn't even crossed his mind. Always before, he'd been so careful. For so long, every relationship he'd had with a woman had been purely one of mutual convenience, and he'd made certain he took no chances.

He had no intention of being a womanizer like his father. He hadn't wanted a woman to put demands on him. He didn't need complications in his life.

He still didn't. But he'd taken Rachel without a thought of protecting her. Why? Even now all he could see was Rachel with a baby. With his baby. He was stunned into silence. He didn't want children. His brief moment of joy was just a latent male reaction.

"What do my letters say, Cody?" Rachel asked as if she knew that he needed time to assimilate her explanation.

"You sure you want me to open them?"

"Sure, I have no secrets. Maude usually does it for me."

Grateful for the distraction, he picked them up. "The first is a letter from the bank. You're overdrawn. And your mortgage payment is late. The second is a payment book for"—he examined the booklet again and swore—"a payment book for your loan on the building on the river."

"How much is the payment?"

"Three hundred and four dollars, due the fifteenth of the month." Razor replaced the payment book and laid it on the table. "Rachel, did you know about this? Were you aware that Harry had mortgaged this property he put in your name?"

"Yes, I signed the papers."

Something about her voice halted him from reaching for her.

"You signed the papers? When?"

She was sorry that she had promised Harry she wouldn't tell. She hadn't realized how it would look to Cody. No, that was wrong, she knew that if Cody learned Harry had been there, he might find a way to follow him. And she'd wanted him to stay.

"Yesterday. He brought the papers for me to sign yesterday. I didn't know about the other building until then. But don't worry. He promised he'd take care of the late house payment."

Razor was stunned.

Harry had been in this house and Rachel hadn't told him. A feeling of disappointment swept over him. It seemed that she'd joined in with Harry, scheming to keep him there, protecting Harry instead of helping him. They'd been together in the most intimate way, and she hadn't told him. Why?

Was that why she'd come to his room the night before? Had she only meant to bind him more tightly to her? If she had, it had certainly worked. He felt betrayed. He'd been used.

"I think you'd better know, Rachel, that according to the bank, as of yesterday afternoon, your house payment hadn't been made."

"How do you know?"

"Because I was there—at the bank. I went down to have a talk with them about financing your repair work. I also went to the Historical Society Planning Commission. Can you believe it? I'm promising them that I'll restore your house at the same time Harry is signing your collateral away. That crook!"

"No, Cody. Harry wouldn't do that."

"Harry did. He had you sign papers that could allow you to lose your home. Why, Rachel?"

"He said a friend needed money. He had to help."

"Harry, the good samaritan, the rescuer of the poor and downtrodden. I don't believe that for one minute."

"I don't know why, Cody. Look what he did for me."

"Yeah, well, I'm still having trouble with that. Why didn't you tell me he was here?"

"I—I had to keep you with me, Cody."

A tightness took over his breathing. He'd been right. "Why, did Harry tell you to?"

"Yes, but, no, you don't understand. Wait!" She called out, stopping him as he turned away. "Cody, it's true, Harry told me to keep you here. But that isn't why I came to your room. I came to you for me."

"Sure. And why would you do that?"

In the silence Rachel heard the telephone installer upstairs dialing the phone. She heard him go through a checklist, then fasten his tool chest and start down the steps.

"All done, Mr. Kimble. Everything is working fine. But your cat is acting weird. He's in there making a nest in your closet."

"I'm waiting, Rachel," Cody said after the man left. "Why did you come to me?"

"Because I knew that you'd leave, and I wanted to be with you before you did."

"With me?"

He wasn't going to let her slide through an explanation. He wanted her to confess, ask forgiveness, absolve his guilt for the feelings he was having so much trouble dealing with. Fine, she could do that.

"I wanted you to make love to me. I wanted to lie in your arms and feel you inside me. I wanted, just once, to have someone I care about care about me too."

SIX

Razor spent the rest of the day working on the house. From the sound of his pounding, Rachel understood the fury that simmered inside him. She expected her proud lion to begin roaring at any moment. He didn't even talk to her. Once she heard him using the phone. At lunch he took his sandwich to the back steps and ate it quickly and in silence.

His invitation to take her to dinner seemed forgotten, until he finally came inside and started up the stairs.

"I'll shower and change, Rachel. Our dinner reservation is for seven o'clock."

"We're still going?"

She sounded surprised, even wary. Damn, he hadn't meant to cause her concern. This problem over his physical need for her was his, and he'd spent most of the day trying to figure out how to deal with it.

"Of course. I said we were going out, and I don't renege on my promises."

The tension didn't leave her shoulders. She was working with a small lump of clay. Sometime during her project she'd wiped her forehead, leaving a powdery shadow of gray streaks. She looked like a little girl, a little girl trying to be very brave, and all he wanted to do was put his arms around her and tell her that everything would be all right. But he couldn't.

He didn't have to tell Rachel that he stood behind his word. She already knew that. She slammed the clay on the board, then patted it in reassurance.

Razor knew he'd said it badly and he tried to soften his sharpness. "Don't stand me up, Miss Rachel. I want to have a look at another place that is supposed to be haunted by a pirate. No sense in letting our Captain think he has a monopoly on our time."

He was right. She was on edge. Rachel finally nodded and covered her clay ball with a towel, waiting until he was upstairs before following.

He didn't have to tell her that he was having a hard time dealing with what was happening. She knew. How to make things right was something she hadn't figured out yet.

The evening ahead would be special. At least it would be to her. So far whatever was happening between them had been private and, to a degree, practical. They'd come together because both of them had something the other wanted. Cody expected to use her to get to Harry. And though she tried not to think about it, she was still convinced that through Cody she'd see again. Both needs were fading in a greater need, a physical need that never lessened.

Rachel walked to her closet and opened the door. All her clothes were arranged according to color. The garments that matched were clipped together with old-fashioned clothespins. There was only one dress in her closet that would do for tonight. She'd bought it years ago, when she'd been invited to a fund-raising dinner by a fellow student whose mother supported philanthropic causes. It was made of black chiffon, with a short, sassy skirt that swished when she moved and a bodice of see-through black lace over a natural-colored fabric chemise.

With the dress she donned black stockings and a pair of scandalously high heels. While she pinned up her hair, she practiced walking in the heels. It had been nearly three years since she'd worn the dress or the heels, or gone to dinner with a special man.

She wanted so badly to look good for Cody. She stumbled and swore, grabbing for the corner of her dressing table. After weeks of early frustration after the accident, she'd eventually made herself learn to accept her blindness. She'd had moments of such depression that she had wished the muggers had killed her instead of taking her vision. But never had she regretted her blindness more than she had for the last two weeks.

In her mind she had a picture of Cody. With her hands she'd added to it, but she wanted to see him. And tonight she wanted to look in her mirror and see her own face, to make certain that she was as pleasing as she could make herself. But neither was possible. With a sigh of regret she gave a final pat to her hair and hoped there were no errant strands.

Applying her makeup by touch, she finished with a dusting of powder to take away any shine. She was dabbing on cologne when the knock came on her door.

Taking a deep breath, she walked to the door, opened it, and stood waiting for Cody's reaction.

It wasn't long in coming. He simply jerked her into his arms and kissed her, letting out a long, deep groan. Moments later her hair was down, the pins scattered all over the floor.

"Rachel, Rachel, you're driving me crazy!"

"Good!"

"Our dinner reservation," he said huskily.

"Do we have to go?"

"I think we'd better. Remember what Maude said."

"Maude?" she murmured.

"Maude and—and—the doctor's appointment."

"Oh—" Rachel pulled away, her body screaming in protest. "I guess I forgot. Don't you—I mean couldn't we . . ."

"No I don't, and no we couldn't. We could, of course, but we're not going to. You've got enough trouble without me leaving you—" Razor let out a deep breath.

Leaving you? He might have bitten back the end of his sentence, but she knew what he meant. She kept making today the beginning of forever, and he kept reminding her that it was only a brief pause. There seemed to be nothing she could do to change his mind, and she wasn't clever enough to play games.

"I think you must be a very strong man, Razor Cody," she said as she turned back to her dressing table and began to repair her tousled hair. "Or a very stupid one."

"You're right, on both counts. Rachel . . ."

"Yes?"

"Don't pin up your hair. I like it as it is." He was doing it again. Pulling back, then making some stupid remark that softened the rejection. She was standing before a mirror, a mirror that she couldn't see an image in. He was glad that she couldn't see the pain in his eyes or the frustration on his face.

"It's all right, Cody. I've told you before. I'm not asking anything of you. Shall we go meet another ghost?"

Before he could answer, or decide whether her response was based on instinct or that special second sight, she'd moved around him and out the door into the corridor, stumbling slightly as she stepped on an uneven length of flooring.

"Wait, lean on me."

He took her elbow and started down the stairs, his western boots making their own echo in cadence with the sound of her heels. He was hugging the wall so that she could hold the banister, but his mind was despertely trying to gear down the urge to forget dinner, pirates, and protection. This time it was Razor whose step faltered. Descending the stairs was as hard for him as it was for Rachel. And it had nothing to do with shoes.

"I'm told that the Pirate House hasn't changed very much," Rachel was saying. "It's still located on the site of what the original settlers called the Trustees' Garden."

"Sounds like a prison," Razor observed wryly as they walked across the parking lot and around to the front of the wooden building.

Rachel laughed. "The Trustees' Garden is where the founding fathers set out all the plants and trees they were to grow in the colony. Hold me tight, Cody, I don't want to fall on my face in front of half the city of Savannah."

"You won't. You're with your knight on a white horse."

"I think," she said as she snuggled into the curve of his arm, "I think I like my lion better."

It was all he could do not to turn around and drag her back to his truck, where he could give in to the urgent impulse to kiss her again. To focus his attention on something other than her delicious scent and the curve of her neck, he searched for innocent conversation.

"The Historical Society gave me a history lesson about the mulberry trees that used to be here."

"That's right. The settlers were supposed to grow them for the silkworms that would produce silk. Unfortunately the trees didn't do well, and neither did the silkworms."

"They were in the wrong place at the wrong time," Razor said. *Like me*. The trees and the worms didn't survive. Razor wondered if he wasn't heading for the same fate.

The hostess met them inside the foyer of the dark, noisy restaurant. The establishment had dining tables tucked into every corner, and like children playing a cheerful game of Follow the Leader, Rachel and Razor trailed their hostess through a series of rooms that opened one onto the other.

With Razor holding Rachel's shoulders and guiding her along, they reached a table in the corner of the large dining room without a misstep.

Razor assisted Rachel to her chair, then declined the wine list. He'd already made one unsuccessful attempt to forget the lovely Rachel by drowning himself in beer. Tonight he needed to be in complete control of his faculties.

There was only one problem. One of his faculties seemed to have its own agenda. At least the corner was dark, and he and Rachel were seated across from each other.

"Tell me about the resident ghost," Razor said.

"That would be Captain Flint. He was the pirate Long John Silver named his parrot after."

"Wait a minute. Long John Silver was a charcter in *Treasure Island*, not a real pirate."

"I know. Robert Louis Stevenson was very creative. Too bad Captain Flint wasn't."

"How was that?"

"He lost his treasure, claimed someone stole it from him."

"Maybe that's the treasure your friend Jacques is searching for. Has he been here?"

"Oh, yes. He even wanted me to come with him,

to see if I sensed anything. Before you ask, I don't." *At least not about treasure*, she could have said.

"So, what happened to the old boy?"

"According to one of the trusted old servants in the inn, he heard a real row upstairs and found the old captain, 'a tossin' and turnin' in bed.' There are still employees who swear they hear him up there, calling for rum and accusing somebody of doing him in for his gold."

They were eating their soup when the head of the Planning Commission stopped by.

"Good evening, Miss Kimble. I'm Winston Phillips, from the Planning Commission. We were glad Mr. Cody dropped by. We're looking forward to his carrying out his plans for refurbishing your house. He seems to have a good grasp of what we require."

"Ah, yes. Cody is working very hard."

"The Historical Board is pleased. Have a good evening."

Rachel inched her fingertips across the table, deftly working around the glasses and other impediments between her hand and Cody's. "Thank you, Cody."

The next visitor was the banker, who cleared his throat and announced his presence. "Miss Kimble. Richard Tharpe, here, First American Savings.

Good to know you've found financial help. Evening, Mr. Cody."

By the time he left, Rachel felt tears begin to well up. She slipped her free hand into her lap for the napkin and dabbed at her lips and the corners of her eyes.

"You didn't have to do that, Cody."

"Of course I didn't. But after what your uncle did to you, somebody needs to see to your interests. Remember the Fool in your cards?"

"I remember."

"Well, I can't be sure whether he represents Harrry or me."

"Not you, Cody. You're my knight on a white horse in a storm, remember?"

"Speaking of storms," Razor glanced out the window beside his chair, "I think that little tropical disturbance is sending us a warning."

"Is it raining?"

"No, but according to the weather report, the storm is moving rapidly toward the coast. It hasn't hit land yet, but we're going to get rain and wind."

Rachel's hand was still clasping Razor's. He liked the way she didn't hide her interest. She was leaning forward, her eyes lowered enough so that when she looked up at him they were fringed with dark lashes that gave her an intensely pasionate look.

Razor swallowed hard. They were carrying on

one conversation about the weather with their vocal cords while their nerve endings were sending a message about a different kind of disturbance.

"Tell me about yourself, Rachel. What did you do as a nursery-school teacher?"

"I worked in a special private school where the children were encouraged to learn many things. Some were taught music. Some learned foreign languages. I played with them and loved them so they wouldn't feel afraid."

Loved them so they wouldn't feel afraid. Yes, Rachel would do that. She'd give to others what she needed, love and reassurance, what he'd once needed so badly. But there was a difference. Rachel was still giving, and he'd stopped asking.

Later, as they left the resturant, Rachel couldn't have said what she ate. She was full of the knowledge that Cody cared enough about her to take on the city and the bank on her behalf. To her that didn't sound like the actions of a man who was only passing through.

Was his need for revenge enough to keep him in Savannah? Had he become her champion and her lover as a means of making certain that she'd allow him to stay? Was he still using her to get to Harry, as he'd said?

No. She might not know what his plans were, but whether he knew it or not, Razor Cody *was* her knight on a white horse. He was a good man who cared about people. He'd shared his past with her, and she'd known, even as he was telling her about his mother's illness and his father's desertion, that he hadn't shared those personal hurts with anyone.

"Lean on me," he'd said, and given a part of himself to her because she needed him.

When he stopped by the pharmacy on the way home, she knew why. When he took her to her room and undressed her, she helped him. When he opened the small paper bag and dumped out its contents, she heard the clatter of multiple packets hitting the dresser and smiled.

Cody might say he was leaving, but the number of thumps said he wasn't in a hurry.

Either that or he was a man who believed that practice made perfect.

Perfect sounded good to Rachel.

And it was, better than she'd ever dreamed.

During the next week Razor completed his written plan for the restoration of Rachel's house. He submitted it to the housing commission and, without waiting for their approval, started making the repairs he could afford.

Any rational person would have demanded answers from Rachel, answers about Harry, about her special psychic abilities, even about the cat. But every time Razor started to ask, he kissed her instead, and nothing else seemed important. In between her clients coming for private readings, Rachel and Cody worked together on removing the peeling wallpaper from the foyer, spending hours doing a wall that should have taken half that amount of time.

Rachel eventually had her appointment with the doctor, who gave her a prescription for birth control pills and cautioned her that they wouldn't be effective for a time. After learning about her problem with her eyes, he called in the eye specialist from across the hall. He checked her eyes and confirmed there was no reason for the continued blindness.

The tropical disturbance named Belle had stalled east of Tallahassee.

Razor spent some of his dwindling supply of funds on hiring a local private detective, who determined that Harry hadn't come to Savannah by train, plane, or rental car. He could find no record of his staying in any of the motels or bed-and-breakfasts, and none of Rachel's neighbors had seen him arrive or depart, either this time or when he'd first brought Rachel there.

In short, Harry was as big a mystery as their ghost.

Rachel managed to come up with the money for

the October house payment and to cover her overdraft. But November was only a week away, and Razor was becoming more and more angry with his ex-partner. Leaving Razor holding the bag was one thing, but throwing Rachel to the financial wolves was another.

She'd been working in her studio all morning while he'd been considering the offers he'd had to take on outside repair work. If he were going to stay and see that Rachel's house was restored, he was forced to find outside income. The most reasonable project was the house on the next block. Plans had already been drawn up and approved; it was simply a matter of carrying out their wishes. He'd called two of his best men in New Orleans and arranged for them to gather up their tools and come. Now all he had to do was find a way to add to his own equipment.

His thoughts were interrupted by a knock at the back door. Dropping the restoration plans, he went to answer the summons. There was a familiar green van parked by his truck, and standing on the porch was a man who was so handsome that even Cody was impressed. He had perfectly tanned skin, perfect white teeth, and a perfect lazy smile. He stilled his raised hand and studied Razor with a frown before speaking.

"Who are you?"

"I'm the carpenter. Who are you?"

"I'm Jacques Devoe. I've come for a reading, but if you're the restoration expert, I'll talk to you first."

"About what?"

"About the construction of these old houses."

"Why?" If Razor had thought Jerry was a threat, this man was an explosion ready to happen. Devoe looked taken aback, but only temporarily, before he replied.

"I believe that there may be treasure hidden in some of these old houses."

"Oh, you're the treasure hunter. I've been meaning to talk to you too. Do you expect Rachel to help you find it by reading the cards?"

"Not necessarily. But I do believe that spirits guard the secrets of their pasts. Secrets could be treasure, and psychics have extrasensory perception."

"Who is it, Cody?" Rachel had moved into the kitchen.

"Your client. He's come for a reading."

"Oh, Jacques. Come on in. I'm sorry. I let the time get away from me."

"No problem. I've been doing a bit of detective work in the neighborhood. Did you know that your house once belonged to a notorious pirate?"

For the first time in days a blast of cold air swept down the hall and slammed against the back of

Razor's neck. *So, you've come back, have you my red-headed Captain?*

"Yes, I know about that old tale," Rachel said quietly, "but I've never been convinced that it was true."

Rachel's client walked past Razor, turned, and looked back, then stepped into the parlor as Rachel switched on the pink-fringed lamp and sat at her work table.

"You've never sensed a presence here?" he asked.

"Ah—no. And I would if there were someone here."

Razor saw the lampshade move as Rachel's client sat. Under the guise of moving his tools to the porch, Razor lingered in Rachel's studio. There was something about the man that bothered him, and it was obvious that he bothered Rachel as well. Otherwise why would she have lied about Captain Perine? Unless she truly didn't feel his presence.

How could that be? Why would he specifically make himself known to Razor and not to Rachel? Then the visitor's question caught Razor's attention.

"Rachel, today I'd like us to do something different. I want you to do a reading about your house."

"I've never done a reading for a house before,

Mr. Devoe. I don't think that would work. There has to be a mental connection between the reader, the client, and the cards. There must be questions to be answered, questions posed by the client."

"All right, then, my question will deal with the house, specifically with Captain Perine."

"Why are you interested in Captain Perine?"

"Because from all accounts he had a great deal of treasure, gold and jewels. He intended to present the treasure to his new wife. A ship believed to be Perine's was recently discovered off the coast of a small island in the Caribbean. In it was a chest filled with precious jewels."

"Then you must already have found his treasure."

"No, according to a diary left behind, the English beauty he married was promised more—much more."

The cold air circulating around Razor seemed to intensify. The cat suddenly appeared, weaving her way around Razor's ankles in a frenzy.

"I'm very sorry, Jacques, but I don't think I can help you. The house doesn't give off any special vibes about a treasure. Perhaps you'd like to cancel the reading."

As if he realized that he was frightening Rachel, Jacques gave a light laugh. "No. I'd still like to go through with the session."

"Fine," Rachel said, but Razor could tell that she was rattled. "Shall we begin?"

Following the same procedure as she had with him, Rachel directed the man she called Jacques to shuffle and cut the cards, then read the name on the cards she turned up. Razor couldn't be certain whether or not Mr. Devoe realized Rachel's distress, but Razor did. She was stumbling in her reading, her hands trembling, her lavender eyes troubled as she sought to understand what the cards were saying.

Finally she stood, dropped the cards, and shook her head. "I'm sorry, Jacques. I seem to have a dreadful headache. The cards aren't clear, and I'm afraid I would be misleading you with my interpretations. It must be pressure because of the storm."

"The storm?"

"Yes, Belle. It will hit the Georgia coast soon. Please come again after the storm has passed."

"No," he argued. "I think that isn't it. You see something," he said. "The cards told you that there is treasure in this house or on the grounds, didn't they?"

"No, the cards rarely tell me anything that specific. I can only give you general answers, and it's up to you to apply them to your question."

"Perhaps," he said with a threat in his voice. "Perhaps you'll reconsider what you didn't tell me.

I'll return, Rachel. After the storm. We'll talk again. I will know what you know."

With that he was gone, leaving Rachel standing behind her table, tilting her head as if she were honing in on a signal.

"What's wrong, sweetheart?" Razor came to her side and put his hand on her shoulder.

Sweetheart? He'd called her sweetheart. But even that didn't take the danger away. For there was danger—for Cody. Jacques represented a threat to Cody. She hadn't known what the cards meant, but she felt the power of unleashed passions. This time they were connected to Cody.

"Nothing," she answered, her voice weary, "at least nothing I can be certain of. I think you're right, you'd better go, Cody. Leave here."

"Leave? What the hell does that mean?"

"It means you're in danger."

"What kind of danger?"

"I don't know. I can't bring it into focus. But it's out there. I can feel it."

"Jacques—the treasure hunter. Is it something to do with Jacques Devoe?"

"No—yes. I'm not sure. Not directly, I don't think."

Razor turned Rachel and put his arms around her. But this time she didn't melt against him as she had before. This time she was stiff and unyielding.

"All right, Rachel. I don't begin to understand your special gift, but I believe that you believe I'm in danger. Sit down. It's my turn to make you a cup of tea. Then we'll talk."

"No. I'm afraid."

"I'll protect you."

But it was Cody who needed protecting. "Turn on the radio, Cody."

He did as he was told, listening as the static on the station announced the approaching disturbance before the announcer's voice came into focus.

The U.S. Weather Bureau announced this morning that the tropical storm Belle has been upgraded to hurricane status. The storm has veered toward land and appears to be heading for a spot somewhere between Savannah and Charleston, South Carolina. Stay tuned for further information. Meanwhile those of you along the waterfront should take precautions and prepare for evacuation.

A blast of cold hit Rachel, and the sudden smell of the sea. She might not have been sure about the interpretation of Jacques's cards, but she'd been right about Cody, right about his being in danger, grave danger.

And then she understood.

The danger was not from Jacques but from Harry! He'd insisted that she keep Cody there any way she could. Cody was being threatened because of her.

Cody had tried to warn her about Harry, but she wouldn't listen. Now it was all coming clear. Harry had used her to draw Cody to Savannah for some reason that she couldn't begin to understand. Even Cody's reading hadn't seemed that ominous. Obviously she'd made a mistake in interpretation. She had to get Cody out of danger—now!

Before it was too late.

But she didn't have to see his face to recognize his stubbornness. He wasn't about to leave.

"Belle is going to hit Savannah, Cody." Rachel said with such conviction that he didn't even try to argue. "You have to get out of here."

"So, we'll do what the announcer said, we'll take precautions and prepare to evacuate."

"Not *we*, Cody—*you*!"

"Sure. I'm going to pack up my goody bag and drive away, leaving you here with a ghost, a treasure hunter, and a fat cat? Not in this lifetime, babe."

Rachel searched her mind for a logical rebuttal. There didn't seem to be one. Everything was coming apart. She was about to lose her house and the man she loved.

Love. She hadn't counted on that. The sisters had loved her, or so they said, but it was impersonal. For so many years her life had been void of any caring. How could she have fallen in love with this stranger, this man she'd never seen?

Because of his goodness. Because he'd obligated himself to take care of her and make her life secure. Because he was her eyes and her soul, that part of her that had been missing until he came into her life.

Now he was going to die.

"No! I won't allow it," she said.

"So, we won't take precautions and we won't evacuate. I think you're far enough inland that you'll be protected from water damage. How often does the Savannah River flood?"

"I don't know. Not since I've been here. But storms come up the river, and the wind damage will be severe."

"The building on the river!" Cody exclaimed. "We probably ought to board that up."

"I don't know where it is. The first I knew about it was when the bank sent the payment book."

"I know. I took a little walk down by the water. The storm won't hit before late tonight. We'll go by Grossman's and stock up on food. Then we'll take the lumber I intended to use here and go board up your building."

"No, Cody. I don't want you in that building."

"What have you seen, Rachel?"

"Nothing! It's just a feeling. The tunnel is dark

at the end. I always knew that. I just didn't know what it meant."

Razor was beginning to get a bad feeling as well. Rachel was convinced that he was in danger. Her conviction was beginning to get to him. Maybe all of this was some kind of giant plot. He'd wondered at the time why Harry had appointed himself as the person to bring down the Caribbean dictator for whom they'd built the hotel. It had seemed a pretty elaborate plot to hatch for humanitarian reasons.

"I don't think you do, Rachel. And even if you do, I'm not going to leave you. Right now, I'm going down to board up your building on the river. Are you coming with me or staying here?"

Rachel didn't know what to say. But she knew that she couldn't let him go anywhere without her. She couldn't stop what was coming, but she wouldn't let him face it alone.

"Let me get a wrap."

Moments later they joined the crowd at Grossman's, where they stocked up on batteries, canned goods, bottled water, and foods that didn't require refrigeration.

"Do you have any idea what kind of building this is?" Razor asked.

"Not a clue. I've never ventured far from my beaten path. All I was ever told is that it's on River Street, away from the Waving Girl."

"Waving Girl? *Waving* is appropriate anyway. Can you hear how the wind is picking up? Papers are flying everywhere."

She could hear, and every gust became a reminder that the end was nearing. "The Waving Girl is a bronze statue of a real girl who lived in a lighthouse on Cockspur Island," Rachel said, trying desperately to focus on something other than Cody's danger. "For forty years she waved at every ship that passed, waiting for her fiancé to return."

"Did he?"

"No, but she never gave up."

Razor was concentrating on finding his way to the river. Turning left on East Bay, he took the first steep side street to the water's edge. The Savannah was already kicking up frothy waves.

The tree limbs were swinging back and forth, and the leaves were blowing in sharp little whirlpools of air current.

The riverboats were heading upriver to ride out the storm. Along the shore, merchants were covering their glass windows with plywood. The promenade was practically empty.

Razor turned left and drove slowly until he spotted the building. With the truck lights shining on it, he could see the vague outline of a name.

"What kind of building is it, Cody?"

"It's a warehouse, Rachel. And it's very old. I can almost read the letters on the front."

Rachel closed her eyes and concentrated. The scene was forming that familiar little vignette on the screen of her mind. "Yes, I see it too. I think it starts with an *F* or maybe it's—yes, it's a *P*."

"It's a *P* all right, followed by six other letters. I believe the original name on the building was Perine's."

Razor killed the engine and leaned back against the seat of his truck. This was really beginning to get weird. A sharp gust of wind sawed off the limb of one of the live oaks to the side of the building and sent it flying through a window on the second floor.

"Well, there's not much doubt about who it belonged to originally—our Captain R. B. Perine."

"I don't understand," Rachel said.

"Well, you own it now," Razor went on. "Obviously Uncle Harry wants you to have it, so we'd better protect it while we figure out what all this means. Let's start by covering the windows with plywood."

But Rachel didn't answer. She was seeing more than the name; she was seeing a man inside the building, a man who was afraid.

"What's wrong, Rachel?"

"I'm not sure. There's someone inside."

"Now?"

"Yes. No. I'm not sure." She closed her eyes and opened them again, but the vision was gone.

"We'd better check it out. I'd hate for some vagrant to get boarded up in there and be trapped."

Razor climbed out of the truck. "Stay here, let me check out the building."

"No! Not without me. Wait, Cody!"

But he was gone, leaving Rachel behind, alone. Her worry turned into fear as she remembered her premonition of danger to Cody. Now it came hurtling through the silence in waves of urgency. The man inside was desperate. Cody was in there with someone who would harm him, and it wasn't Harry.

Rachel started to slide from the truck. She had to get to Cody. As she tried to get her bearings, she heard footsteps returning. The truck door opened, and a hand jerked her inside.

"Cody?"

He didn't answer, only started the engine and drove the truck quickly away.

"Cody, was anyone there?"

Only silence. Rachel acknowledged what she'd known from the moment the door was opened. The man sitting beside her wasn't Razor Cody. The man beside her was the danger she'd felt, the fear, the darkness at the end of her tunnel.

"I demand that you get out of this truck immediately!"

"It's too late for you to demand anything, my dear Miss Kimble. You might have been in a position to do so if you'd cooperated. But you chose not to. Now you'll have to give me the answers I want, whether or not you wish to do so."

"Jacques? Is that you?"

"But of course."

"Where is Cody?"

"He's in your building."

"Why?"

"To get him out of the way."

"What are you doing here?"

"Looking for Captain Perine's treasure. The treasure he stole from my ancestor."

"I don't have any idea what you're talking about, Jacques. I can't help you. I'm not clairvoyant. I'm not a spiritualist. I simply read the tarot cards. Sometimes I interpret them correctly, sometimes I don't."

"But you know. I could look at your face and tell, Miss Kimble. You may only read the cards, but your sight is much deeper. You see with other senses."

"What did you do to Cody?"

"Let's just say that he interrupted my search. I didn't think the treasure was there, but I had to make certain."

"And it wasn't?"

"No. Still, without him, I may yet accomplish

my goal. With Cody as my prisoner, I expect you'll tell me what I want to know."

"Prisoner? Have you hurt him?"

"No, other than a rather large lump on his head, he's fine. I expect he's taking a nap."

"What are you going to do with me?"

"I'm going to take you home of course. Then you will make me some tea and we shall conduct a séance."

"No, I refuse."

"I think you'll change your mind."

"Not until you go back and get Cody. I can't help you find any treasure. I don't know how to conduct a séance. I'm not a spiritualist."

"I know, Rachel. But, you see, I am."

SEVEN

Razor woke to total darkness and the eerie sound of wind.

His head ached, and there was something wrong with his arms, no, not his arms, his hands. He couldn't move them. As he struggled, a tingling sensation ran up his muscles toward his elbows. Even his shoulders trembled.

Something had happened, something bad. He tried to pull reason back from the chaos of sound, find a thread of light in the confusion that rolled through his consciousness.

There was a tightness at the edge of his face just above his ear. It hurt when he moved and crinkled with stiffness as if he'd spilled paste on himself. Perspiration beaded up in his hairline and dribbled down his face, bringing with it the faint odor of blood.

Blood. Someone was hurt.

Rachel!

With a groan he willed himself, through sheer concentration, to still the vibration in his head and the ringing in his ears. Only then did he know that his feet didn't work right either. *Open your eyes, Razor. See where you are. You have to find Rachel.*

Wherever he was, the building was moving, swaying as if something were pushing against it. There was a crack, and he heard something falling in front of him. He blinked. His eyes were open, open to total blackness.

"Help!"

But the only sound came from the creaking of the building in the wind. Someone had tied him up! His hands had no feeling.

Gradually, in fleeting snatches, blurred moments of memory came back. He and Rachel had gone down to the river in search of Harry's building. They were going to board it up against the approaching hurricane.

Rachel. He'd left her in the truck while he went inside. How had he gotten in?

The door—yes, the door had been open.

It hadn't been so dark then; there'd been some kind of light. He'd called out, "Hello? Is anyone here?"

His voice had echoed through the building.

Then he was in a large, open room, a storage area probably, for there were dusty boxes and rusted drums. In the half-light he could see the floor, see footprints leading inside.

"Harry? Is that you? Don't play games with me, you low-down, miserable cheat!"

Razor hadn't stopped to think, he'd simply charged into the darkness, tasting the pleasure of getting his hands around Harry's neck and throttling him. Finally Razor Cody would get his revenge.

Razor groaned. He'd been a fool. Why had he expected Harry to be there? He should have used caution, reconnoitered the area. Razor hadn't even seen his attacker, only felt the sharp blow to the side of his head. His last conscious thought was that Harry had outsmarted him once more.

But the man hadn't been Harry, and Razor was still alive. He moved his feet and discovered that they weren't tied nearly as tightly as his hands. It was the boots he was wearing. They'd interfered with his assailant's attempt to immobilize him. Quickly he began to work his foot from the boots. No luck. He needed to plant one boot behind the other to anchor it.

If only he could find a table, or a wedge of some kind. The moaning of the wind was growing louder, and he thought he heard the sound of rain clattering against the roof. Hurricane Belle was drawing closer. And Rachel was—God only knew what had happened to her.

Razor slid forward, working his way around a box, then a fallen beam. As he tried to right himself, he realized that he'd found his wedge. Sitting on the dusty floor, he moved ahead until he could cup the toe of his boots beneath the beam. Then, an inch at a time, he pulled his feet from the boots.

He was free. At least his feet were. Now to get his hands loose. Until now he'd resolutely refused to allow himself to think about who would want to harm Rachel. For she had to be the unknown assailant's goal. If he'd been the intended victim, the attacker wouldn't have stopped with a blow on the head.

There was a crack in the boarded-up window of what must once have been an office. If there was any glass left, he could free his hands. Moments later, with only a few mislicks, he'd used the jagged edge of a pane to cut away the binding. After he'd untied his hands, he quietly pulled on his boots and made his way toward the front of the building.

Just as he reached the door, he heard a swooshing sound, and part of the roof on the building flew off. The storm was growing fiercer.

"Rachel?" He charged out the door and lunged into the wind, ready to take on Harry, or anyone else who might be waiting.

In his heart he'd known she would be gone. With her second sight she'd have been in that building if she could have, blind or not. The street was empty. Rain was being driven at an angle toward the river, which was now slinging whitecaps toward the shore.

His truck was gone.

And so was Rachel.

The blood was his.

Rachel tried not to think about what had happened to Cody. Instead she concentrated on getting away from her captor. She'd free herself, then go back for Cody.

She wasn't sure where they were until he parked Cody's truck and forced her up the steps at the back of her little house.

Witchy didn't come to the door to meet them as they entered the kitchen. Rachel, accustomed to the darkness, could have found her way without faltering. Instead she reeled against the counter, the kitchen chairs, and caught the garbage can with her foot, sending it sprawling, anything to distract the man.

"Cut that out, Miss Kimble. You're not going to get away!"

He slammed her into the chair beneath her fringed lamp and dragged his own chair close to her side. From the warmth overhead she could tell that the light was burning, though from the sounds of the wind and the tree limbs hitting the house, she wasn't certain how long it would be before the electricity would fail.

She needed to stall him, delay whatever he had in mind. If she could keep him occupied until the power went off, she might have a chance to escape. But how?

"Mr. Devoe, I don't know what you have in mind, but I'm soaking wet and I need to take off these clothes."

"Believe me, Miss Kimble, I'd like nothing more than to undress you, but that comes later. Now I have more important things on my mind."

"What?"

"Treasure. I've narrowed my hunt to your house. The treasure has to be here. That's the only thing that accounts for Captain Perine's presence in the house."

"You're crazy. There are ghosts in most of the old houses here. There are slaves and widows and even a child or two. Are they all protecting treasure?"

That stopped him for a moment. Now, if she could just keep him off guard.

The building groaned. Rachel managed to chatter her teeth in a reasonably authentic shiver. "I'm sorry. I can't seem to make any sense out of what you're saying. I'm too chilled."

"I can't see how you could possibly be cold. The heat and humidity are oppressive. However, I'll light the fire if that will enable you to concentrate."

"No! No fire. Not with a storm coming. It could burn the house down."

"You're right. I don't want this house destroyed until you tell me where the gold is."

Rachel was very tired. And she was worried. Where was Cody? What had this odious man done with her knight on a white horse?

"What gold, Mr. Devoe?"

"The gold that belonged to Captain Flint."

That caught her by surprise. "Your ancestor was Captain Flint, the rum-soaked old pirate who is supposed to haunt the Pirate's House? I thought you were French."

"My father was. My mother was an Irish girl who was a direct descendant of Captain Flint, and his treasure belongs rightfully to me. Your Captain Perine was a thief."

"Of course he was, but he isn't my Captain Perine, and I don't believe a word of this."

"It doesn't matter. I believe it. I found a map."

"Captain Flint must have left hundreds of treasure maps. Most pirates did, and most of the maps were phony."

"Yes, but my map led me to this house."

"I don't believe it. And even if it were true, what makes you so sure I can help you? Don't you think if I knew where any treasure was, I'd use it to help myself? You really are crazy."

"That was a mistake, my dear." He grabbed her wrist and twisted it painfully. She felt his hot breath on her cheek, and this time her shiver was real.

"I've been called crazy for years, ever since I learned I had a talent for reaching the spirit world, but *I* know better. And before this night is over, so will you."

"What—what have you done with Cody?"

"You mean that carpenter who thinks he's your protector? I wouldn't count on any help from him. If that old building survives the storm, I'll be surprised."

"He isn't dead, is he?"

She asked the question, knowing the answer. Cody wasn't dead, but he was in pain. She'd felt it, her head aching unbearably for the last few minutes. Cody was alive, but there was something wrong. He couldn't move. Maybe he was paralyzed. She had to get away from this lunatic and back to Cody.

Rachel jerked her arm away and stood, darting toward the front of the house. She didn't even reach the foyer before Jacques hauled her back into the parlor and slammed her down into the chair.

"Now, stay put. If I can't trust you to do it, I'll force you." The sound she heard was familiar, but she didn't know what it was until he slid his belt around her waist and fastened her to the chair back.

She was trapped in a storm with a crazy man, and the man she loved was hurt and in pain.

Oh, Captain Perine, if you are a real ghost and you're anywhere around, I need your help now.

But there was no answering tilt of the table. The floor didn't move, and no spiritual voice came out of the darkness. Rachel wasn't going to get any ghostly intervention. If she was going to help Cody, she'd have to do it on her own.

"All right, Jacques. I've already told you, I don't know anything about séances, but I'll do it—if you'll let me go afterward."

"I thought you'd see it my way."

"You'll have to tell me what I have to do."

"First it's too light in here. Do you have candles?"

"In the drawer next to the refrigerator."

"Matches?"

"On the mantelpiece."

While Jacques was setting up the candles, Rachel slid the belt buckle from the back of the chair to the front. Once it was dark, she'd free herself. Then what? She cursed her blindness, allowing a rush of suppressed self-pity to wash over her.

It wasn't fair. One act of kindness had left her blind and destroyed her life. She'd never been lucky, and she'd learned not to expect it. When the doctors had explained that her blindness was caused by the blow to her head, she'd accepted it as another in a long line of painful events to befall her. Then they'd told her that it could be temporary. Her sight could return at any time.

She never told anyone about those first hours of darkness and pain; how it had intensified until she'd wanted to scream. How suddenly the pain had stopped and she'd felt as if she were falling. Then somewhere out in front of her there'd been a strange kind of light. From out of that light a man had come forward. He'd been tall and dark, wearing a fierce scowl that had forced her back, away from the light. He'd kept walking toward her, pushing her back with his hand. When she felt the warmth of his touch, she lost her fear.

And she'd backed away, eventually waking up in the hospital where she'd learned that she was blind. Later she'd found that she often saw things, had a sixth sense that showed her visions. She'd continued to see the man whose frown had sent her back. In time she'd come to believe that when he came again, her sight would be restored.

When Cody arrived, she'd felt that warmth again. She'd been so certain that Cody was *the* man, her knight on a white horse. Now she could cost him his life in return for saving hers.

Jacques Devoe returned to the table, and Rachel heard the click of the switch as he turned off the overhead lamp. "There, that's better," he said.

"Does the room have to be dark to hold a séance?" Rachel asked.

"Not totally, but almost."

"Now what happens?"

He slid his chair forward. "Now we hold hands."

His hands were clammy.

"Now we concentrate," he said in a low voice, "and allow the spirits to feel comfortable with our presence."

Rachel didn't speak. She barely moved as she searched frantically for a way to break away.

"You're too jumpy! Be still. Empty your mind. Let your thoughts run free."

Rachel concentrated on being still. If there was a spirit in the house, she hoped it was the Captain and that he'd rescue her from Jacques Devoe. But nothing happened.

"O spirits of the night," Jacques whispered, "know that we are waiting. We beseech you, come to us, tell us of the mysteries we seek to understand. Come . . . Come . . . Come."

Not even Witchy's meow broke the silence.

Rachel's hands began to cramp. Her shoulders tightened. And then it happened. A sudden feeling that they weren't alone, a sensation of being watched. A cold lick of air brushed against her cheek. "Oh!"

"What? What is it?" Jacques asked impatiently. "Do you see something?"

"Hardly," Rachel managed to speak. "I'm blind, remember."

"Be quiet! He's here. I know it. He's here in the room with us right now."

"Who?"

"Captain Perine. And he's angry."

"How do you know?" Rachel asked, though she didn't really need an answer, for she felt a presence as well. But it wasn't anger that swirled around the room, it was confusion and sadness and the sensation of expectation.

"I told you. I'm a bit of a psychic myself. I've attended enough sessions to know when spirits are present."

"Then why do you need me? Just ask the spirit what you want to know and go."

"It doesn't work that way. Spirits don't always cooperate unless there is some connection to the person who is asking. Now, stop talking and concentrate. Once you've established the connection, you ask the spirit for help."

"Me? Why me? I'm not the one looking for treasure."

"No, you're trying to save your carpenter before the storm blows him away."

"What have you done with Cody?"

"Just made certain that he doesn't get out of that building on the river. And from the sound of the fury blowing up outside, I doubt that the building will survive. So you'd better hurry."

This time Rachel didn't doubt him. If it took communicating with the spirits to save Cody, she'd talk to the Devil.

Concentrating all her mental capacities on reaching the spirit whose presence she sensed, she said, "If there is someone here, I earnestly ask for your help. Tell me what to do to satisfy this man who threatens to hurt someone I love."

With a roar of fury the wind swept through the bay window, shattering the glass and catching Jacques Devoe's chair in its fury. Rachel heard a crash and a yell, then as suddenly as the wind had come, it stopped and there was silence.

"Mr. Devoe?"

There was no answer.

"Captain Perine?"

There was no answer.

Carefully Rachel unfastened the belt holding her to the chair and stood. She took a step and heard the crunch of glass beneath her feet. The rain blew through the window, pelting her face with stinging moisture. Making her way toward the back door, she tried without success to open it. It seemed to be blocked.

The phone. She'd call somebody. Following the wall, she made her way around the room until her foot hit something. She leaned down and touched it. Jacques!

The man was truly evil, but she didn't want him dead—not in her house, not because of her. She ran her fingertips up his back until she located his neck. Placing her hand against his carotid artery, she felt the beat of his pulse. He wasn't dead, just out cold.

Stepping carefully over him, she made her way to the phone, lifted it, and dialed 911. But nothing happened. The phone was dead.

Rachel felt tears of frustration roll down her face. "Damn it to hell! It isn't fair. I can't see. I can't call anyone for help. And the man I love is about to be blown away in a hurricane!"

She slid down the wall and sat there in the darkness, crying out loud for the first time since she was a very little girl.

Then she heard a welcome sound, a cat's meow. Witchy was somewhere in the house calling to her. Rachel turned her head in one direction, then the other. "Witchy? Where are you?"

The sound continued. Perhaps Witchy had been hurt, trapped somewhere by the storm. Cody, herself, now Witchy. There was nobody to do anything except her, and she was blind.

Rachel struggled to her feet and listened again for the cat's cry. She didn't need to see, her mind's eye could guide her. As she made her way toward the cat, she heard another blast of wind slam against the house. More glass shattered. There was a sound as if someone had stumbled, then footsteps.

Jacques? Cody?

She couldn't be sure.

Rachel slipped into the closet at the foot of the stair and pushed her way to the back to wait. She was greeted by a satisfied meow, and the closet door slammed shut. She heard the ominous snap of the lock. After a moment she tried to turn the knob. It didn't move. She and Witchy were trapped inside.

EIGHT

Razor Cody made his way around the van parked at the corner and away from the river up Abercorn Street. The wind was blowing in such gusts that he was forced to hold on to trees, streetlights, statues, any stationary object he could find.

Sometimes he'd be blown back and have to fight his way to where he'd already been long minutes before. The whole world turned murky, smeared with streaks of darkness and pain as the lights went out one by one. Razor felt as if he were alone in a world of wind and sound, as if nature had lost her way and, like some frightened child, was lashing out.

And underneath it all was fear. Fear for Rachel, the same kind of fear that he'd held tightly leashed when his father had deserted him and his mother, fear that had intensified during his mother's illness until he could no longer deal with the terrifying knowledge that he would be left alone. He'd closed it off, shut away the pain, and used his fear to propel himself forward, every accomplishment a further reassurance that he had control over his own destiny.

None of that mattered now. For Rachel was in danger. As her knight on a white horse he'd been a miserable failure. He'd loved her from the first moment, but he'd refused to admit it, refused to accept the love of a woman who wanted someone to care for her as much as she cared about him.

The sound of the storm increased. Sweeping gusts of wind came from one direction, then changed and slammed in from another. Paper, limbs, garbage cans were being tossed about like Frisbees, and there was no one to catch them.

There was constant agitation, noise alternating with sudden silence as though the storm were catching its breath to gear up again. It did, this time clipping a utility pole and slamming it like a battering iron into one of the huge old live oaks. Both crashed to the ground, leaving sparks of fire dancing about from the wires writhing like snakes on the ground.

This was the kind of storm that had taken down pirate ships, with shrieks of fear from the sailors on board. Razor could almost hear their cries, almost feel their fear. It must have been a night like this when Captain Perine's vessel went down, taking him to the bottom of the sea.

Razor stopped, trying to get his bearings. He was still on Abercorn, but more than that he couldn't be sure. Above the fury of the storm he heard a cry. "Rachel?" No, that was impossible. The sound was inside his head. But he heard her. She was calling for help.

As another swell of moisture-laden air pushed him forward, Razor caught at a knee-high object in his path. It was stone, granite perhaps, and square. He clutched at the object, feeling the imprint of letters beneath his fingers. Words.

Where was he?

Then he identified his anchor: a tombstone. He was in the cemetery in one of the small parks near Rachel's house. He'd passed it earlier on his way to visit the Historical Society.

Historical Society. He let out a wild laugh. They'd been so worried about keeping the houses true to the time, and now they were all in danger of being blown away.

There seemed to be no boundary to the storm. The tree limbs thrashed with a crashing sound that was immediately caught up by the wind and swallowed in its frenzy. Razor waited for the occasional lull and dashed forward, picking his way through the debris and downed power lines like a drunk reeling in a blinking strobe light.

One block closer to Rachel.

What if she wasn't in the house? Suppose the man who'd taken his truck had kept on driving? That couldn't be. The connection that had snapped into place that first night was even stronger now. With certainty he knew Rachel was somewhere ahead of him. Whoever had been in the building had stolen her, and it had to have something to do with that treasure hunter.

Razor hadn't seen his attacker, but he knew with calm certainty that it was Jacques, not Harry who'd taken Rachel. The man was a lunatic. He was convinced that there was treasure to be found in Savannah and that Rachel was the one who would lead him to it.

What if she failed?

What if this creep hurt Rachel?

Harry no longer mattered. Reputations and businesses could be rebuilt. Razor didn't want to think what it would mean to lose Rachel. "Bless you, Harry," he whispered. "If it hadn't been for your manipulations, I'd never have come here and I wouldn't have found Rachel, wouldn't have fallen in love with her, wouldn't be here now to—do what?"

Suddenly, as if on command, the storm hushed. As if he were coming out of a deep, dark pit, Razor looked around. He was just where he thought he was, on Rachel's block. Taking off at a mad dash, he reached the lane behind her house and let out a great sigh of relief.

His truck was there. The intruder had brought Rachel home. She was safe. Or was she? At that moment the back door opened, and a man staggered down the steps and into the yard.

"Hold it right there, buddy!" Razor called out, heading toward the man.

"Get away from me!" the man screamed as he pushed past Razor and into the street.

The man was Jacques Devoe. Razor let him go. For now he had to find Rachel. As Razor climbed the steps to the porch, he heard Jacques's scream and saw the flash of light. He'd stepped on a live electrical wire.

Razor charged into the house just as the storm struck with fury once more. "Rachel! Rachel, where are you?"

The power was off, and the sound of the wind and rain masked his cries.

She was there. He could feel her presence, somewhere, somewhere hidden. Up the stairs and down again. He leaned against the post at the bottom of the steps and concentrated.

Where are you, my love?

And then he heard the cat's meow, coming from the closet opposite the steps.

Razor opened the door.

"Cody?"

It was Rachel. She was safe.

Razor dropped to his knees and pulled her into his arms. If nothing else good ever came into his life, he'd at least have this moment.

"I tried to get back to you," she sobbed, "but I got locked in here."

"Rachel, you're all right?"

"Oh yes. Where is Jacques?"

"I'm afraid he's gone. I think he was—scared to death."

"He called out to the spirit world, Cody, and I think he finally found it."

"Our Captain?"

"I don't know. I'm so glad you're safe. I was afraid."

"So was I. It's pretty rough out there."

"The world sounds as if it's being destroyed."

"Some of it is." He leaned back against the closet wall and pulled her down with him, not relaxing his hold as he adjusted her in his lap. "Devoe didn't hurt you?"

"No. He only wanted me to help him find his ancestor's treasure."

"His ancestor? Who?"

"It seems Jacques is related to Captain Flint of the Pirate's House, who just happened to be a seagoing buddy of our Captain R. B. Perine."

"Are you sure he didn't hurt you?" He was touching her all over, as if he had to make certain that she was still in one piece. His hands touched her cheeks, her eyebrows, and her mouth.

"I'm sure. What about you? I know something happened to you."

"How . . . ? No, never mind. It's that second sight of yours. What did it tell you?"

"That your head was hurt." She ran her fingers up the side of his cheek until they reached the spot above his ear. "Here."

Razor flinched. "That's the spot, all right. Devoe creamed me with a stick of wood, tied up my ankles and my hands. I think he must have followed me. Does he drive a green van?"

"He drives a van, but he never said what color it is. Aren't you cold? You're wet all over."

"I suppose I could take off my wet clothes," he said with a chuckle. "But what would happen if someone came to check on us?"

"Nobody's coming," Rachel assured him as she began to unbutton his shirt. "Besides, we're in a closet filled with cast-off overcoats and other garments."

"And one beautiful woman."

"And a cat."

"Cat? Where is the yellow-eyed voyeur? I suppose she's going to sit in the corner and watch us get blown away together?"

"No, she seems to have disappeared. Apparently there's an escape hole somewhere behind some of these boxes." Razor's shirt was gone, and she was reaching for the button on his jeans.

"No fair, you're getting a head start." He pulled the peasant blouse down, kissing her neck and the tops of her breasts, the skin warming noticeably as he skimmed her shoulders with his lips. "I wish I could see you," he whispered.

"I'm glad you can't. We're even now. Both of us are blind."

"My darling, Rachel, all the way from the river I thought of nothing else but you and me, and what a fool I've been, how blind *I've* been—about everything."

"You came back for me. You might have been killed." She hushed him with a kiss.

His hand touched her breast, circling her nipple, touching almost reverently. The storm outside raged, feeding the electricity that darted between them, shooting sparks like the live wires he'd danced over as he'd made his way to Rachel. This time he didn't try to avoid the heat. This time he welcomed the rapid heartbeat signaling that her desire was as great as his.

Razor still didn't believe what had happened between them. He wanted to touch her, every part of her, to give. But he didn't know how. He'd been with women, but they were only women he'd taken for mutual pleasure. They'd known what they wanted and hadn't been shy about asking.

Rachel? Miss Rachel Kimble was gentle and rare, and he wanted to cherish her. Summoning what little fraction of control he had left, he removed her bra, her panties, and her skirt, moving slowly, ignoring the throbbing of his manhood as she unzipped his jeans and pulled them down his body.

"I'm glad you weren't," she murmured.

"Weren't what?"

"Killed. I couldn't have stood that, to come so close to heaven and have you fly back there, to the light, away from me."

Her voice was throaty, echoing across the closet. There was a silence inside that seemed at odds with the wind and the rain beating against their house.

"You might be better off," Razor said in a voice so tense that he wouldn't have recognized it as his own.

Rachel pressed herself against him, finding the curve of his arm as she laid her head against his chest.

"I've been waiting all my life, Razor Cody. I just didn't know who I was waiting for, until you came. And I believe that you've been waiting for me."

"Did the cards tell you that?"

"No, my heart told me. Can't you feel it talking to you?"

He moved his hand to the place where her heart ought to be and felt the pulse beating rapidly beneath her breast. Every nerve ending in his skin felt and absorbed the sensation of her response. Then his fingers moved lower, setting off corresponding currents as they slid lower and lower.

He heard her gasp when he reached the apex of her thighs. She was half lying over him, her body pressed against his knee. He pulled her forward, settling her between his legs. His fingers crept lower, seeking the source of her heat, the moisture that made her satin smooth, that coaxed sweet sounds from his lips and arched her back as he entered that chamber of warmth.

"Oh, Cody," was all she could say, over and over, "Ohhh, Cody . . ."

He focused on her voice, on the twitching movements of her body, on her soft giving as she opened herself up to him, giving all.

He didn't have to have light to know she was beautiful. He didn't have to know the words to understand her song of love, for he, too, felt the music.

Hot, throbbing need stung his loins, testing his body's control. He was holding back, forcing himself not to take, waiting until she was ready and asking. There was no more confusion. He closed his eyes and pulled her forward until she was over him, until he was pressing against that fervent heat, until she, impatient with his restraint, pushed herself down with unexpected longing.

And all question left his mind. There was only one way to get past his wanting and that was to open up and let his love run free. He wanted to belong to Rachel, to take her, over and over, loving her with every part of him and being loved in return.

He'd expected climax. He'd expected joy unbounded. But the depth of their explosion was astonishing. As was the joy and contentment that came later as he held her in the darkness.

"Do you think the house will survive, Cody?"

"I think so. People built houses to last back then. That's what I like so much about these old structures."

"How long will the storm rage?"

"I'm not sure, several more hours, I'd guess."

"Good." She leaned against his chest and pulled his arms around her. "I want to be as close to you as I can for as long as it lasts."

"What do you know about Harry?" Razor was still holding Rachel, though they'd pulled coats from the rack to build a bed and cover themselves.

"Not much at all. I was sitting in the solarium one day when he first found me. I could smell the crisp scent of the sea around him, and his pipe tobacco."

"Did he give you any explanation of how he found you?"

"No, only that he'd been searching for me for a long time. He'd been with my father when he died, and Father had made him promise to look after me."

"He was your father's brother?"

"So he claimed. But I never knew for sure. When my father left my mother, he went to sea. Harry said that once Father had tried to find me, but we'd moved and he didn't know where to look. By that time I was with the nuns."

"But Harry found you. How do you explain that?"

"I can't. How do you explain his finding you? I think that Harry considers himself a brother to every man. I sometimes think that he is too good to be real."

Real? Razor digested that thought for a moment, then allowed reason to prevail. "Now, wait a minute. Are we talking angels here? I don't buy that for one minute. Angles don't do deliberate harm to people."

Rachel felt the tension return to Cody's body. She might believe in things that couldn't be seen or proved, but Razor wasn't about to—not yet.

"Not even," she ventured, "when the harm results in a greater good?"

"But he ruined my business, my reputation. I even served time in jail."

"That's true. But because of you an evil dictator was brought to justice and money was returned to the people who needed it most. I found a home, and what's even more important, my darling Cody, because of Harry you found me."

"No. I refuse to believe in angels, guardian or otherwise. Harry was a flesh-and-blood crook who bought this house and took out a mortgage on your building on the river. Angels don't do that. Ghosts don't do that. Honorable men don't do that!"

As if in reproach, the storm came roaring to life with a vengeance. It slammed against the house, caught the wooden shingles on the roof, and slung them away like bullets from a machine gun. For one moment there was a giant shudder, then a snap as something was ripped from its place and smashed against the closet. This time the wall didn't survive. The beam fell across the space where Cody and

Rachel were hiding, striking Rachel across her head and pinning them down inside.

"Rachel! Rachel!" Razor called out to the woman he was holding. But she didn't answer. He could feel her heart beating, feel her breath as it fluttered against his neck. Desperately Razor tried to push the beam away.

The mahogany stair support with the strange carvings along the base. He wasn't about to move anything that heavy. Maybe he could slide out. But every move elicited a moan from Rachel. He couldn't hurt her more.

"Ah, Harry, if you're responsible for this, you've really done it. Rachel is hurt, and I can't get us out. I said I was going to shave your head, then cut it off. I may forget the shaving and go straight for the knife."

Gradually the wind hushed, leaving only the rain, which threw a spray across the two lovers trapped beneath the rubble. Throughout the night Razor held Rachel, whispering words of love and promises of a future together.

The rain stopped sometime before morning. When Rachel finally opened her eyes, the sun was beaming through a hole in the roof. And Cody was—Cody—

"Razor?" Her voice was soft and filled with wonder.

Razor jerked awake. "Rachel? Are you all right?"

"Oh, Razor, you're beautiful. Just as I saw you in my vision."

She was kissing him, and he was returning her kisses hungrily when her words finally worked themselves through his joy that she was awake. "'Beautiful'? What are you saying?"

"Oh, Razor, I can see! You came to me, and now I can see."

She leaned as far away from him as she could, running her fingertips across his forehead, his eyebrows, his lips and down, pausing at the tattoo above his nipple. "You're so beautiful—so very beautiful. Stop frowning. I love everything about you. Cody, I can see you. Thank you."

"I didn't have anything to do with that. It must have been the lick on your head—from the beam, the storm."

"And now the storm is over. I can see the sun. Oh, Razor, look at all the reflections of color."

Razor was having a hard time looking away from Rachel's beautiful face. There was a puffy red mark across her forehead, above her eye. But that was the only blemish on a face so filled with life and love that he could only marvel at what he was seeing.

Then a particle of gold drifted across her face and away, striking the wall and bouncing off again. The remaining walls of the closet were studded with tiny particles of color. Maybe they were both hallucinating.

"What is it?" he asked.

Rachel lifted her head, following the beams of bright light from the roof to the floor outside the closet. "Cody, look. Look! It's the treasure. We've found Captain Perine's treasure."

Across the hallway, scattered like pieces of broken glass, were hundreds of colored stones, spilling from the base of the oddly shaped beam that made the last rail of the stairs. The gems refracted the light into a million dancing sparks.

"Devoe was right all along," Razor said in disbelief.

"And so was Harry. He promised he'd provide a way to pay for the house and that he'd send me someone to share it with."

Razor didn't argue. He'd run out of arguments. As he'd held Rachel through the night, he'd come to understand that success measured through Rachel's eyes was success of the heart. What had happened to bring him there no longer mattered. The only thing he cared about was this woman and what they could give each other.

"Okay, Captain," he said, "I'll concede. You want me here, I'm here. But if we're going to keep this treasure a secret, we need to get out before somebody comes to check on us."

But it wasn't the Captain who provided their escape, it was Witchy, who clawed her way in from the back of the closet, pushing boxes away to reveal missing panels torn from the rear of the closet.

"Meow?" She stood in the opening for a moment, then as if disgusted with her charges, flipped her tail in the air and disappeared.

By the time Maude pounded on the door, they'd managed to slide around and out the hole into the parlor. They'd dressed and dragged an old-fashioned trunk down from the attic. As if it was meant to be used for that purpose, the trunk now held the Captain's treasure of diamonds, rubies, pearls, and emeralds.

"Are you all right?" Maude burst into the house, carrying Petey under her arm.

"We're fine, Maude," Rachel answered. "We're more than fine. Oh, Maude, I can see."

"Your vision returned?"

"Just like the doctors said. Of course, being conked on the head by a beam may have helped."

Maude stood, looking from Rachel to Cody and back again. "I'm glad you're okay. The district has been damaged, but not as badly as it might have been. The worst of the storm hit those old buildings by the river. They're pretty much gone."

"Oh, Maude, not Riverwalk."

"No, those on the other end, the unrestored warehouses."

"Your building, Rachel," Razor said.

"The only fatality was that treasure hunter," Maude went on. "He stepped on a live wire."

Rachel gasped. "Jacques, poor Jacques. He never knew that he was right about Captain Perine."

"And you were right too," Maude said, her voice revealing her awe. "You said you'd regain your sight."

"Because of Razor," Rachel said quietly.

"No, I can't claim any credit for that," Razor said. "It was the storm."

"So what happens now?" Maude asked, turning to Razor. "I don't mean to pry, but Rachel's house is going to need massive repair. Does this mean you're prepared to stay?"

Say yes, Rachel. Say you want me to stay. Say I'm still important to you.

Razor listened for Witchy to meow. She didn't. He waited for a lick of cold air to slide across the back of his neck. None came. He waited for Rachel to answer. She only stared at him in confusion.

Finally he said in a half statement, half question. "What about it, Rachel? What do you see in the future?"

When Rachel raised her gaze to meet his, there was a questioning tilt to her head. Her eyes were frosted in silver, turning lavender eyes to blue. Her brow furrowed. Then she let out a long breath.

"I'm afraid it's gone, Cody. There is no more second sight, no seeing with my mind's eye. All gone. I'm just like everybody else now. I'm an ordinary person again. I can take care of myself."

Razor knew it was over. The fantasy, the illusion, the special dreams, all locked away in a trunk with Captain Perine's treasure.

Maude soon left, but the wonder Rachel and Razor had shared seemed to have blown away with the storm, leaving awkwardness where there'd been none.

"I guess you won't need me now that you have the jewels," Razor said.

"I guess you can restore your company and get on to bigger projects," Rachel said.

"I guess. But, before I go, I'll try and get this mess cleared out so that you can get around. I should have figured out about the beam; it was so clearly out of place here."

"I should have known. I had the gift. Every time I touched it, I sensed something. I didn't understand."

Only when Razor wrenched the broken beam away from its base did he see the rest of the Captain's loot, bars of gold stored in the base.

"Oh my, Rachel, look at this." Razor lifted one

heavy bar, examining it carefully. "Redbeard's gold."

"Gold? He had gold as well?"

"Well, someone did. There are initials scratched along the bottom. No, not initials, I think it says Flint."

"Not the Captain's, but Flint's gold. Poor Jacques. He'll never know that he was right about the gold. It really belonged to him. And Harry," Rachel added. "We'll have to share it with Harry. If it hadn't been for Harry, we wouldn't have any of this. The truth is," she said quietly, "none of this belongs to us."

Razor returned the gold to its hiding place. "You're right. I came here for revenge, to make Harry pay for the wrong he'd done. Taking part of the treasure without facing Harry just isn't the same."

"You could always stay on. I mean, sooner or later Harry will return. I'm sure of it." *Don't go. I want you to stay—for me.*

"I suppose I could, and while I'm waiting, I could get your house fixed."

"We could use what we need and put the rest back in the beam—for Harry."

Razor eased the beam back to the floor. He slid his arms around Rachel and considered his answer carefully. What he was about to say would commit him for all his life, which wouldn't be long enough to do all the things that a real knight on a white horse would do.

"Maybe this knight wants to do things on his own, save his lady in his own way. I let Harry help me once because I was impatient, ambitious, determined to claw my way to the top any way I could. I don't think I want to do that again. Using this treasure is like accepting Harry's help. I think I'll pass."

"But Razor," Rachel argued. "I don't think we ought to be foolish. It's here and we found it. Why not make some good come of all of this? We don't have to profit, but we could provide other things people need, like nursery schools and mulberry trees."

"Mulberry trees? But they didn't survive, remember?"

"Only because our founding fathers didn't have you, Cody, and they didn't have Harry. You have to stay, Cody. I figure that between the three of us anything is possible."

"You aren't afraid that we'd lose the treasure?"

"We could always ask."

"Ask who?"

"The tarot cards. After all, they haven't been wrong yet."

"Ah, Rachel, you know I don't believe in that

stuff. And I don't believe in ghosts either. I'm the master of my own fate."

Rachel smiled up at the scowling man who'd come into her life bent on revenge. "Oh, yeah? How else do you explain what's happened?"

"I don't. I can't. I don't understand any of this."

What Razor did know was that he'd intended to use Rachel to force Harry to return everything he had lost. But she'd give him so much more.

He told himself that Rachel had used him to bring back her sight, and now that sight exposed the ugly things in the world. What she'd seen before, with her special gift, was beauty of the soul. Otherwise why would she ever have wanted him?

Rachel had read the cards, and she believed that the cards had given answers that promised fulfillment. In their own way, he guessed, the cards had been true.

"Please?" she asked.

"But," he snapped, not yet ready to give in to something he couldn't understand, "your cards didn't answer my question."

"What question?"

"I believe it went something like, 'Where's Harry?'"

"Do you still care?"

Razor looked at her, watching the lavender return to her eyes as she waited for an answer that was so much more than a question about Harry.

"No, I don't think I do," he finally answered.

"Then take me up those steps and make love to me, Razor Cody. In the sunshine, where I can see everything I've been feeling."

Making love to Rachel wouldn't give him answers. But maybe there weren't any. Maybe there were some things that had to be accepted on faith. Like Harry, and Witchy, and Rachel.

He didn't believe in those cards, but he believed in Rachel. If ghostly intervention had brought them together, who was he to argue? He lifted Rachel in his arms.

The lick of cold that hit Razor from the rear removed the last vestige of his doubt and shoved him up the steps. The door closed emphatically behind them, and Rachel began a wickedly physical explanation of what they were doing, examining every move and every reaction as if she were discovering a treasure more priceless than the one they'd found in the beam.

For the rest of that afternoon Miss Rachel Kimble didn't need to rely on the tarot cards. She could interpret quite well without them.

NINE

The sheets were rumpled and the air was heavy with the perfume of love. Rachel sat, one leg curled beneath her, as she shuffled the tarot cards.

Razor leaned against the one pillow left on the bed and watched the woman he loved. She'd said, sometime during the afternoon, that she'd never seen beyond his arrival. In her special visions there'd been no future, no forever after. There had been the two of them, together.

Maybe that was all she'd needed to see. Razor had never believed in fantasy, in second sight, or the unknown. Yet how else could he explain what had happened? At some point question and disbelief had fled, being replaced with the quiet confidence of Rachel's love.

Now there was a vitality about her that had been absent before, an energy that seemed to intensify every time they touched. Where she'd once appeared gentle and serene, she fidgeted, worrying with her hair, pursing her lips as she studied the cards until she pulled one from the group and placed it in the center.

"I'm not sure this is a good idea, Cody. When I said ask the cards, I meant about Harry. Fortunetellers don't read their own cards."

"Why not? If you're only telling what the cards mean, how can it matter who you're doing it for? Is this card you?"

"No, this card is us."

She laid out the card called the Lovers. "I'm reading our future, Cody, just as I read yours."

"Our future?" He liked the sound of that.

"Yes," she said positively. "I don't know that it will work, but if I'm going out on a limb, I'm going to have company."

"I like the sound of that. And speaking of company, don't you think we'd better combine our questions and change our position if we are emulating our card?"

"Our card?"

"The Lovers. They aren't sitting across from each other. Come over here, love."

He opened his legs and pulled her between them, her back against his chest, his chin resting on her shoulder, his arms clasping her abdomen.

"Now, deal. If I don't like the cards you choose, we'll cheat."

Rachel gave out a gasp, not so much from the thought of cheating but from the erratic dance of her pulse as he cuddled her. This was not going to work. This was not a good idea.

He nibbled on the side of her face, planting kisses with lips drawn into what seemed to be a permanent frown. "Now, Rachel, what is to be our question?"

"Ah, yes, the question. I say that we each pose a question, secretly, without revealing it. The answer given by the cards is always open to interpretation by the asker."

She was trying to be totally serious, holding the cards against her breasts, every part of her held stiffly, waiting for his answer. She was right. His major question was no longer, Where's Harry? His question was, Does she love me?

"All right," he agreed, "if you think that it will work."

"It isn't a question of what I think, Cody. It's a question of what you believe." *I already know that the cards will reveal truth to my question: Can I make him love me enough to stay?*

Rachel leaned forward, momentarily creating a space between them as she laid the Lovers card in the center of the sheet. "I'll shuffle them. Now, you cut them three times to the left."

Cody followed her instructions, forcing his mind to concentrate on the cards rather than on the way Rachel's long golden hair swung forward and caressed her breasts.

He took a deep breath and handed the cards back to her, allowing his fingertips to linger for a moment against the soft underside of her wrist.

"This card covers us," she began. "It presents the climate in which we now exist."

"The climate in which we now exist? I think, my lovely fortune-teller, that our climate is pretty obvious, and if it isn't, a few more movements will make it so."

"Stop it, Cody. This is serious." She turned up the Four of Swords.

"Okay, Miss Rachel, what does it mean?"

"Rest after war, relaxation from suffering, a change for the better."

He gave a disbelieving laugh. "You mean like now, after making love for most of the afternoon? Yeah, I could buy that."

"Perhaps. Or maybe it's referring to the storm, or what happened. As I said the answer is there for you to interpret. Anyhow, I think it's fair to say that discord is behind us and we're free to enjoy our time together, however long or short that may be."

However long or short that might be? Razor knew how he felt, but he wasn't certain about her. Did she still expect him to go, even after suggesting that he wait around for Harry?

The next card was called the Empress. It pictured a regal woman sitting on a red throne. She was wearing a big crown and carrying a scepter. One leg of the throne was a heart with some kind of symbol inside. Razor felt a sense of relaxation.

"Who's the royal babe?" He pulled Rachel back against him, breathing in the smell of her hair, reveling in the feel of it against his chest.

"The Empress crosses us. She reveals the opposing forces and determines whether they mean good or evil."

"Like in Star Wars? May the force be with you."

Rachel tilted her head up and gave him a tentative smile. "Do you see the symbol of Venus? That's the circle inside the heart, with the cross below it. That represents womanhood, fertility. If I were giving a reading to a woman, I'd tell her that the time was right for her to conceive a child."

"A child?" Razor felt a pang of guilt. The packets he'd bought were still on the top of the bureau. He'd said there were some things for which there were no explanations, things you accepted on faith. Loving Rachel was one of them.

From the first time they'd made love, he'd behaved in a totally irrational manner. He'd bought condoms, then left them on the nightstand. He'd refused to think of Rachel except as a temporary diversion, yet he'd done the one thing that would mean he'd have to stay.

He'd fallen in love. His hands cupped Rachel's belly and he felt a sudden warmth that flared for a moment, then disappeared as she shifted her position. He didn't have to ask the question, he knew the babe with the big crown represented good.

"This card can either represent marriage or material wealth. It's up to the reader to determine which future the asker is truly seeking. You have to decide."

Rachel gave the proper answers, knowing even as she spoke that she already had hers. The only wealth she wanted was what she'd just shared.

"Why can't I have both?"

Rachel couldn't voice an answer. With Cody's rough hands cupping her stomach, she was having a hard enough time remembering what the cards represented.

"The third card," she said quickly, "is beneath us. This represents something that is already part of our experience."

"I like the 'beneath me' idea. Couldn't we put the reading on hold?"

Rachel ignored him and turned over the next

card, the Three of Pentacles. "Upside down. Not good, but at least it's past."

"What's not good? I can tell you from personal experience that there isn't anything about us that isn't good."

"The card tells of lack of skill, of selfishness, preoccupation with gain, neither of which apply to you, Cody. You're the most unselfish man I've ever known, and your skills are obvious. This has to apply to me."

"Rachel, my darling, you are bursting with skill. Look at the lesson you just gave me in visual appreciation of the body. If that isn't enough to convince you, what about your figurines and your tea?"

For a second Rachel allowed herself to relax against him, reveling in the feel of his strength. *I never knew about making love before. You taught me, Cody. You've brought out a part of me that I didn't even know existed.*

"As far as that preoccupation with gain you're talking about, I guess we both know that's me and my ambition," Razor admitted. "I'm sorry, Rachel, about holding you responsible for my losses."

"That's both of us. You wanted to regain your company. I wanted to see again. We were both preoccupied with personal gain. The next card is something that is just passing away."

Razor recognized the next card. Strength. The

beautiful woman, petting the lion. "I've seen this card before. You said I had the strong spirit of a lion."

"Yes. Funny, I never thought I was strong. I guess we're both strong people when we have to be. You came to me through a storm."

"Good over evil. My, that sounds a little scary. But I think I believe the force-of-character bit. That's another way of saying the strong survive while the weak perish."

His voice was rough. The fingers caressing her stomach had tightened into fists. The truth was, the entire reading was too close to the truth. He was still worrying over his question. Did she love him? She hadn't said she did.

"This card crowns us." Rachel started to turn over the card, caught sight of the Five of Cups, and halted her movement.

Razor found himself reaching out, clasping her hand so tightly that she winced. "Don't be afraid, Rachel. We can handle it, whatever it is." He took the card and laid it in place.

"Maybe," she said, the print of his fingers still etching her wrist. "What this card stands for is yet to come. It can mean disappointment, sorrow from the things from which pleasure was formally taken."

"Not making love. As long as that stays the same, I can deal with anything else."

"Do you mean that, Cody? We could be in for some pain."

"What could possibly be more painful than what we've come through? Think about it, Rachel. You lost your family, your job, your sight. I lost my family, my business, and my future. When we met, we'd had our pasts erased. We have a blank slate. We survived, and our future is up to us."

She didn't argue, but she knew that only one thing would make her future right—Cody's love. And she didn't know how he felt about her.

"I don't know, Cody. Before, I didn't expect anything. Before, I had nothing, so it didn't matter. Now . . ."

"My beautiful Rachel, you're seeing the glass as half empty. I happen to know it's half full. Stop being sorry. What does the next card say?"

She turned over a reversed Nine of Swords and relaxed her frown. "Maybe you're right. This card tells us what is going to happen. It represents patience, healing, an end to suffering."

"See, it just takes faith."

Razor never expected to hear himself building a future. He was talking about half-full glasses. Having faith. He sounded like his mother. And it didn't bother him. Because it came to him suddenly that those little remarks had been her way of making it easy on her son. She'd draw her concerns into one positive statement and share it with him. Then she'd laugh and for a few moments, her pain would seem better, better for having given way to a stronger emotion—love.

That's what he'd lost so long ago. That's what Rachel had given back to him. Love and a future.

"Faith," Rachel repeated skeptically, and leaned back against Cody. Maybe he was right. Maybe their positions had reversed. He was seeing glasses half full while hers were half empty. She didn't know when the change had occurred. Before she'd only been afraid for herself, and because she was helpless to change anything, the fear was a kind of comfort. Now that comfort was gone. She had to make choices and she had to face a different kind of pain.

Cody planted a kiss on her cheek, a gentle kiss that spoke of new understanding, of healing and promises. "The Lovers, remember? We're in this together, however it turns out. Let's see what we have in store."

Rachel leaned forward and turned over the first of the four cards that would forecast their future, the Five of Swords, reversed.

She let out a little laugh. "'Beware of pride,' the card says. There is a very good chance that we will lose something very important." There was a long pause. "Both of us fear that."

"The treasure?" Razor said quietly. "I've been

thinking about that, Rachel. I think we ought to put it back in Harry's beam. Use only what we need and leave the rest. I'm not sure I trust anything that Harry sent. I built a business before, through my own hard work. I can do it again."

Rachel nodded. Razor immediately thought of losing their treasure. It was reasonable that he would think of treasure, and just as reasonable that her fear was of losing him.

"How many more cards?" he asked. "When do we get to the answer to our questions?"

"Three more cards. The next one is family opinion."

"Well, that lets us out. We have no family, except of course your Uncle Harry, if he is really your uncle. What does good old Harry say?"

Even Razor didn't have to be told that the card she laid out was the Devil, nor that her look of dismay was very real.

"I don't think I want to do this,Razor."

"Why, are you afraid that we'll see old Harry's true colors?"

"I don't want you to be right about him."

"Would that be so bad?"

"I think it would be."

Razor's arms tightened about her, holding her close, giving her reassurance with his touch. "But it's too late to go back. You've already revealed the card, haven't you?"

He was right. It had been too late from the moment she'd opened the door and invited him into her life. She'd wondered once if he was the man she'd been expecting, the man she'd seen in the tunnel of darkness. He was. She hadn't had to wait for the return of her sight to know that. Every touch had reaffirmed their connection.

"Yes. This card tells about the influence of those around us. The Devil—black magic—use of force and evil."

"Wow! That's pretty tough stuff. No chance that it could be reversed in some way?"

"No. And the sad thing is that maybe the card is right. It's sensuality without understanding. Satisfaction without knowledge of the consequences."

Razor rubbed his face against hers, trying to fathom a reasonable meaning to the card's prediction. There had been instant sensual awareness and there'd been satisfaction beyond his greatest expectation. But there was more between them, and he refused to accept that it was based on anything but good. Any evil that existed came from Harry, or Jacques, or some force that didn't stand a chance in hell of surviving now that he knew what it was to love someone.

"Okay," he said calmly, "so we know what we

think and what those around us think. What's left?"

Rachel held the cards against her chest and studied those already laid out. She wished it was the previous day and she couldn't see, that it was the previous week when she was still rejoicing in the wonder of Cody's arrival, when she was discovering that the man who pretended to be so tough was really soft and caring inside.

But it was too late to go back. The cards had brought them together, and now they'd have to play out the ending.

"The third card in the forecast reveals what we hope for. Justice. And it's reversed. Justice reversed."

Razor studied the card. The character was some kind of high priestess, wearing a red robe, sitting on a purple throne. She was holding the sword upright, as if she were challenging the asker.

"What does she say, Rachel?"

"She represents hope against injustice, inequalities, complications."

"I don't understand. If you were reading for Maude, how would you interpret this?"

"I'd advise Maude that she should temper her actions with mercy and understanding."

Razor ran his fingertips down her stomach, skimming the inside of her thighs. "Mercy and understanding sound good to me," he whispered wickedly.

"Stop it, Cody. Be serious. We only have one card to go, the card that gives us the final outcome."

"I'm not sure I want a card to control us."

"The cards don't control us, Cody, they simply give us possibilities. What we do with them is up to us." She turned the final card over and whispered, "Oh no. The Ten of Wands."

"Wands, as in fairy tales?"

"No," she answered in a dead voice. "This card represents selfishness—power used unwisely—force and energy. Test by fire. Hearts tried by pain."

"And that's bad?"

"That's very bad. Oh, Cody, I love you, and I don't think I can take any more pain. If you're going to leave me, just go—now."

"I'm not going to leave you, Rachel. I'm going to stay right here and repair the roof on this house, finish the restoration, start over again—if you'll have me."

"But why?"

"Because I love you. Because old Harry was right about one thing, you and I belong together."

"We do? But what about the pain and suffering ahead?"

"What about it? I still don't believe all this business about the cards, but there's no rational explanation for anything that's happened. I don't understand how you saw me. I don't understand Harry and why he went to such lengths to bring down a dictator."

"Don't you see, Cody, Harry is goodness. That's all. Everything he does is to right a wrong. I'm not sure of the connection between Harry and Captain Perine, but I don't suppose it matters."

"Rachel, there's something I'd better tell you. I think there is a good possibility that Harry and Captain Perine are . . ." He couldn't bring himself to say they were the same person. Instead he settled for "related."

"What makes you think that?"

"Do you remember I asked what the Captain looked like?"

"Yes, and I told you he had a tawny streaked red beard and red hair."

"Yes, you did. And that description exactly matches Harry."

"But that can't be," she whispered. "Captain Perine is a ghost. Harry can't be a ghost. How did he—I mean how do you explain . . ."

"I don't think it can be explained, Rachel. It doesn't compute. How is it possible that we met? That we fell in love?"

"I don't know. Maybe some things are better off

not being explained. Maybe we'll never know the truth about Harry. Maybe he'll never come back."

"Oh, I think he will. Captain Perine did, and Harry is too good a con artist not to want to meddle in his work. Maybe the Captain wasn't free to go, not until something happened."

"Like what?"

"Well, I'm not certain that I really believe all this, but suppose Captain Perine had to make restitution for his life of crime."

"And it's taken him two hundred years to do that?"

"Maybe it took him that long to make it work. Maybe he had to find someone like Harry to work through. And—well, what about this house? You told me it was once a school."

"But it didn't last. And what about all the people who wouldn't stay here?"

"We know that subtlety wasn't the Captain's way. You did say people kept moving out. What if he had to find the right people?"

"Yes," she agreed, "people who would accept him, who would use the treasure wisely. I could buy that. But that doesn't explain the warehouse on the river. Why on earth did he mortgage it?"

"Maybe that was just some of Harry's con work," Razor added.

"Or maybe he needed ready money. After all, we

hadn't found the treasure yet, and he doesn't seem to have been able to touch it."

"Harry always needs money. Any other ideas?"

Rachel pursed her lips. "I'm the one with the second sight, but I don't have an answer. I think I'll believe that Harry is my uncle and he came because I needed him, just as you did. He filled my glass halfway, and you've run it over."

"I like that, Miss Rachel Kimble."

"So have the cards answered your question?" she asked.

"No, that answer came from you."

"Oh? What is that?"

"I couldn't ask, but I needed to know if you loved me. I'm still not sure I believe it."

Rachel dropped the cards on the sheet and twisted around so that she could look up at this dark, frowning man who'd given her more than she'd ever dared dream. She slid her arms around his neck. "Don't you know? I've loved you since I saw you in that tunnel of darkness so many months ago. I would have died if you hadn't sent me back."

"Tunnel of darkness?"

"I don't know how to explain it, but I was dying. Then suddenly you came out of the light at the end of the tunnel. You frowned at me, forcing me away, making me live. After that I carried you around in my mind every moment until you knocked on my door. Didn't you know?"

"You had one of those out-of-body experiences?"

"I don't know what it was. I only know that you were there and you cared. That's when I fell in love with you, frown and all."

"And I thought those cards were spooky. I'm beginning to think there may be something to all this second sight."

"Except it's gone now, Cody. I don't seem to be able to see anything. Even the cards don't have that connection when I touch them. I've lost all my special sensations, except those I feel for you. I love you, Cody. You're all I need."

"Good. Then my most important question has been answered."

"So has mine."

"What did you ask?"

"I wanted to know that you love me too."

"I thought you knew that in the beginning."

"No," she admitted. "I only knew that I loved you. I still do, always and forever."

"Always and forever. I think I like that. And I'm glad you don't have those powers anymore. If we're going to make this future work, it has to be a normal, regular relationship between two regular, normal people. No revenge. No more ghostly intervention!"

For a moment Rachel felt a draft of cold air sweep around her back. She shivered. "I think it must be getting cooler outside."

"Not in here," Razor said, refusing to recognize that eerie sensation that danced around the room. "There's only us, Razor Cody and his woman. Nobody else," he said evenly, and turned his attention to the kiss she was asking for.

It was early evening when he woke to darkness and felt the second sweep of cold. Rachel was lying on his arm, sleeping peacefully.

Through the window the moon shattered the room with light that was almost as bright as day. Razor lay there, unsuccessfully willing the intruding sensation to go away. It only intensified. Finally he spoke.

"All right, where are you, you old crook? You've convinced me. But I don't intend to spend the rest of my life with you looking over my shoulder."

There was no answer. The cold continued to swirl around.

"I'm still not sure that I believe in ghosts, and I don't know how in hell you could do what you've done, but I'll admit you seem to have pulled it off."

Nothing.

"Harry, you're a peeping Tom. Either show yourself or get lost!"

Then he heard it, an angry meow.

"Witchy? Where have you been, you yellow-eyed witch? I thought the storm must have blown you away."

The cat jumped on the bed and padded across the sheet to Razor's chest. She was carrying something in her mouth, something black and alive.

"If you're bringing me a mouse, don't. I don't want any gifts from you. I don't even like you."

Rachel woke slowly, listening in puzzlement to Razor's conversation. He was talking to someone—something. Witchy?

"No, don't drop it. Wait."

Rachel pulled herself up to a sitting position beside Razor at the head of the bed. "What is it?"

"Well, now I know why Witchy was getting fat."

A squirming little black ball of fur was crawling up Razor's chest.

"Kittens," Rachel said in delight. "So that's why she kept disappearing, why the telephone man said she was building a nest in the closet."

A second black kitten was deposited on the bed, then a third.

Razor looked down at the kittens and shook his

head. "And I was ready to think that there was some kind of connection between this cat, our Captain Perine, and Harry."

"Oh? How?"

"Well, every time either of our red-bearded pirates made his presence known, Witchy disappeared. Seems she was just out courting and enjoying the fruits of her escapades."

"Well, I think she is a very sensible cat." Rachel let out a little purr and stretched serenely. "Every female deserves fulfillment, even the four-footed kind."

"But not in our bed. I refuse to share our bed with anyone but you. Do you hear that, Harry?"

"Harry isn't here, Cody. I wish you'd get that out of your mind."

"I don't trust him. I don't trust Witchy either. If she thinks she's going to bring those kittens up here and disappear, she's wrong. Where are you, cat?"

The answering meow was immediate. The black cat jumped on the foot of the bed and walked slowly across the covers, deliberately dropping the large kitten she was carrying between Rachel and Razor. Witchy gave a triumphant little cry, then stepped back and sat down, her yellow eyes glowing in the darkness.

"Well, this fellow was quite a mouthful," Razor observed as the kitten crawled drunkenly up on his leg, sank his claws into Razor's soft flesh beneath the sheet, and turned his gaze on Razor.

"He's an odd color, isn't he?" Rachel said curiously.

Razor didn't answer. He was getting a bad feeling about this. He'd seen that tawny red color before.

"It can't be," he finally said, his voice tight with disbelief.

"Meow?" *Why?* Witchy seemed to say.

"What?" Rachel added.

"I'll be damned. It can't be."

The kitten's claws dug deeper. And Razor felt the telltale warmth of moisture sink through the sheet and onto his leg. It couldn't be true. None of this could have happened.

Ghosts? Yes, he'd buy that, ghosts of the past, for both he and Rachel. They'd both known the absence of love and the fierce desire to make a life without being dependent on anyone else.

Treasure? Yes, there was treasure, but he knew now that the gold and jewels weren't the prize. The real treasure was Rachel.

Rachel and love.

And he'd give Harry credit for bringing them together, for finding a way to force them to leave the past behind and start new. Why? How? He didn't know. He didn't need to know. Razor pulled Rachel into his arms and smiled, a real, honest, satisfied-with-the-world smile, as he studied the kitten and accepted the truth.

"Razor, you're smiling!"

"That I am."

"This odd-looking red kitten is making you smile? I don't understand," Rachel said. "All the other kittens are jet black. Where'd this one come from?"

"It's simple, very simple. The old crook. He's here, christening my leg. He never really left."

"Who's here?"

Lying there with a woman who believed he was a knight on a white horse, in a house with no roof and a fortune in gold and jewels hidden in a stair rail, Razor Cody's smile turned into a deep, loud laugh that startled all the kittens and brought Rachel closer into his arms.

"Ah, Rachel, my question has truly been answered. We don't have to understand love, we just have to believe."

The tawny kitten gave a satisfied little cry, and years later both Razor Cody and Miss Rachel Kimble would agree that, even in the moonlight, there was no mistake. The kitten had winked.

And there was no mistake in Razor's mind either when he nodded his head and said, "Harry!"

The *Savannah Gazette* reported two unusual items in the paper the following April. An anonymous donor had made a contribution to repair the statue of the Waving Girl, destroyed during the October hurricane. The donation was made jointly in the name of Savannah's two most famous pirates, Captain Perine and Captain Flint.

The second announcement described the wedding of Miss Rachel Kimble and Mr. Reginald Agnew (Razor) Cody, which took place in Lafayette Square. Pink and white azaleas spilled over the garden path in a riotous splash of color. The bride, wearing white, beamed. The groom, wearing black, frowned. The wedding march was played by a group of traveling Gypsies, and the guest list included all the friends whose lives had been touched by the magical aura of love that surrounded the couple.

Scampering among the limbs of the live oak tree overhead were three half-grown black kittens, and, off to the side, one odd-looking, tawny-colored one who seemed to be watching with an expression that could only be described by the reporter as satisfied.

THE EDITOR'S CORNER

Let the fires of love's passion keep you warm as summer's days shorten into the frosty nights of autumn. Those falling leaves and chilly mornings are a sure signal that winter's on the way! So make a date to snuggle up under a comforter and read the six romances LOVESWEPT has in store for you. They're sure to heat up your reading hours with their witty and sensuous tales.

Fayrene Preston's scrumptious and clever story, **THE COLORS OF JOY,** LOVESWEPT #642 is a surefire heartwarmer. Seemingly unaware of his surroundings, Caleb McClintock steps off the curb—and is yanked out of the path of an oncoming car by a blue-eyed angel! Even though Joy Williams had been pretending to be her twin sister as part of a daredevil charade, he'd recognized her, known her when almost no one could tell them apart. His wickedly sensual experiments will surely show a lady who's adored variety that one man is all she'll ever need! You won't soon forget this charming story by Fayrene.

Take a trip to the tropics with Linda Wisdom's **SUDDEN IMPULSE,** LOVESWEPT #643. Ben Wyatt had imagined the creator of vivid fabric designs as a passionate wanton who wove her fiery fantasies into the cloth of dreams, but when he flew to Treasure Cove to meet her, he was shocked to encounter Kelly Andrews, a cool businesswoman who'd chosen paradise as an escape! Beguiled by the tawny-eyed designer who'd sworn off driven men wedded to their work, Ben sensed that beneath her silken surface was a fire he must taste. Captivated by her beauty, enthralled by her sensuality, Ben challenged her to seize her chance at love. Linda's steamy tale will melt away the frost of a chilly autumn day.

Theresa Gladden will get you in the Halloween mood with her spooky but oh, so sexy duo, **ANGIE AND THE GHOSTBUSTER,** LOVESWEPT #644. Drawn to an old house by an intriguing letter and a shockingly vivid dream, Dr. Gabriel Richards came in search of a tormented ghost—but instead found a sassy blonde with dreamer's eyes who awakened an old torment of his own. Angie Parker was two-parts angel to one-part vixen, a sexy, skeptical, single mom who suspected a con—but couldn't deny the chemistry between them, or disguise her burning need. Theresa puts her "supernatural" talents to their best use in this delightful tale.

The ever-creative and talented Judy Gill returns with a magnificent, touching tale that I'm sure you'll agree is a **SHEER DELIGHT**, LOVESWEPT #645. Matt Fiedler had been caught looking—and touching—the silky lingerie on display in the sweet-scented boutique, but when he discovered he'd stumbled into Dee Farris's shop, he wanted his hands all over the lady instead! Dee had never forgotten the reckless bad boy who'd awakened her to exquisite passion in college, then shattered her dreams by promising to return for her, but never keeping his word. Dee feared the doubts that had once driven him away couldn't be silenced by desire, that Matt's pride might be stronger than his need to possess her. This one will grab hold of your heartstrings and never let go!

Victoria Leigh's in brilliant form with **TAKE A CHANCE ON LOVE**, LOVESWEPT #646. Biff Fuller could almost taste her skin and smell her exotic fragrance from across the casino floor, but he sensed that the bare-shouldered woman gambling with such abandon might be the most dangerous risk he'd ever taken! Amanda Lawrence never expected to see him again, the man who'd branded her his with only a touch. But when Biff appeared without warning and vowed to fight her dragons, she had to surrender. The emotional tension in Vicki's very special story will leave you breathless!

I'm sure that you must have loved Bonnie Pega's first book with us last summer. I'm happy to say that she's outdoing herself with her second great love story, **WILD THING**, LOVESWEPT #647. Patrick Brady knew he'd had a concussion, but was the woman he saw only a hazy fantasy, or delectable flesh and blood? Robin McKenna wasn't thrilled about caring for the man, even less when she learned her handsome patient was a reporter—but she was helpless to resist his long, lean body and his wicked grin. Seduced by searing embraces and tantalized by unbearable longing, Robin wondered if she dared confess the truth. Trusting Patrick meant surrendering her sorrow, but could he show her she was brave enough to claim his love forever? Bonnie's on her way to becoming one of your LOVESWEPT favorites with **WILD THING.**

Here's to the fresh, cool days—and hot nights—of fall.

With best wishes,

Nita Taublib
Associate Publisher

P.S. Don't miss the exciting big women's fiction reads Bantam will have on sale in September: Teresa Medeiros's **A WHISPER OF ROSES,** Rosanne Bittner's **TENDER BETRAYAL,** Lucia Grahame's **THE PAINTED LADY,** and Sara Orwig's **OREGON BROWN.** We'll be giving you a sneak peek at these terrific books in next month's LOVESWEPTS. And immediately following this page look for a preview of the spectacular women's fiction books from Bantam *available now!*

Iris Johansen

nationally bestselling author of

THE TIGER PRINCE

presents

THE MAGNIFICENT ROGUE

Iris Johansen's spellbinding, sensuous romantic novels have captivated readers and won awards for a decade now, and this is her most spectacular story yet. From the glittering court of Queen Elizabeth to a barren Scottish island, here is a heartstopping tale of courageous love . . . and unspeakable evil.

The daring chieftain of a Scottish clan, Robert McDarren knows no fear, and only the threat to a kinsman's life makes him bow to Queen Elizabeth's order that he wed Kathryn Ann Kentrye. He's aware of the dangerous secret in Kate's past, a secret that could destroy a great empire, but he doesn't expect the stirring of desire when he first lays eyes on the fragile beauty. Grateful to escape the tyranny of her guardian, Kate accepts the mesmerizing stranger as her husband. But even as they discover a passion greater than either has known, enemies are weaving their poisonous web around them, and soon Robert and Kate must risk their very lives to defy the ultimate treachery.

"I won't hush. You cannot push me away again. I tell you that—"

Robert covered her lips with his hand. "I know what you're saying. You're saying I don't have to shelter you under my wing but I must coo like a peaceful dove whenever I'm around you."

"I could not imagine you cooing, but I do not think peace and friendship between us is too much to ask." She blinked rapidly as she moved her head to avoid his hand. "You promised that—"

"I know what I promised and you have no right to ask more from me. You can't expect to beckon me close and then have me keep my distance," he said harshly. "You can't have it both ways, as you would know if you weren't—" He broke off. "And for God's sake don't *weep*."

"I'm not weeping."

"By God, you are."

"I have something in my eye. You're not being sensible."

"I'm being more sensible than you know," he said with exasperation. "Christ, why the devil is this so important to you?"

She wasn't sure except that it had something to do with that wondrous feeling of *rightness* she had experienced last night. She had never known it before and she would not give it up. She tried to put it into words. "I feel as if I've been closed up inside for a long time. Now I want . . . something else. It will do you no harm to be my friend."

"That's not all you want," he said slowly as he studied her desperate expression. "I don't think you know what you want. But I do and I can't give it to you."

"You could try." She drew a deep breath. "Do you think it's easy for me to ask this of you? It fills me with anger and helplessness and I *hate* that feeling."

She wasn't reaching him. She had to say something that would convince him. Suddenly the words came tumbling out, words she had never meant to say, expressing emotions she had never realized she felt. "I thought all I'd need would be a house but now I know there's something more. I have to have people too. I guess I always knew it but the house was easier, safer. Can't you see? I want what you and Gavin and Angus have, and I don't know if I can find it alone. Sebastian told me I couldn't have it but I will. I *will*." Her hands nervously clenched and unclenched at her sides. "I'm all tight inside. I feel scorched . . . like a desert. Sebastian made me this way and I don't know how to stop. I'm not . . . at ease with anyone."

He smiled ironically. "I've noticed a certain lack of trust in me but you seem to have no problem with Gavin."

"I truly like Gavin but he can't change what I am," she answered, then went on eagerly. "It was different with you last night, though. I really *talked* to you. You made me feel . . ." She stopped. She had sacrificed enough of her pride. If this was not enough, she could give no more.

The only emotion she could identify in the multitude of expressions that flickered across his face was frustration. And there was something else, something darker, more intense. He threw up his hands. "All right, I'll try."

Joy flooded through her. "Truly?"

"My God, you're obstinate."

"It's the only way to keep what one has. If I hadn't fought, you'd have walked away."

"I see." She had the uneasy feeling he saw more than her words had portended. But she must accept this subtle intrusion of apprehension if she was to be fully accepted by him.

"Do I have to make a solemn vow?" he asked with a quizzical lift of his brows.

"Yes, please. Truly?" she persisted.

"Truly." Some of the exasperation left his face. "Satisfied?"

"Yes, that's all I want."

"Is it?" He smiled crookedly. "That's not all I want."

The air between them was suddenly thick and hard to breathe, and Kate could feel the heat burn in her cheeks. She swallowed. "I'm sure you'll get over that once you become accustomed to thinking of me differently."

He didn't answer.

"You'll see." She smiled determinedly and quickly changed the subject. "Where is Gavin?"

"In the kitchen fetching food for the trail."

"I'll go find him and tell him you wish to leave at—"

"In a moment." He moved to stand in front of her and lifted the hood of her cape, then framed her face with a gesture that held a possessive intimacy. He looked down at her, holding her gaze. "This is not a wise thing. I don't know how long I can stand this box you've put me in. All I can promise is that I'll give you warning when I decide to break down the walls."

VIRTUE
by
Jane Feather

"GOLD 5 stars." —*Heartland Critiques*

"An instantaneous attention-grabber. A well-crafted romance with a strong, compelling story and utterly delightful characters." —*Romantic Times*

VIRTUE is the newest regency romance from Jane Feather, four-time winner of Romantic Times's *Reviewer's Choice award, and author of the national bestseller* The Eagle and the Dove.

With a highly sensual style reminiscent of Amanda Quick and Karen Robards, Jane Feather works her bestselling romantic magic with this tale of a strong-willed beauty forced to make her living at the gaming tables, and the arrogant nobleman determined to get the better of her—with passion. The stakes are nothing less than her VIRTUE . . .

What the devil was she doing? Marcus Devlin, the most honorable Marquis of Carrington, absently exchanged his empty champagne glass for a full one as a flunkey passed him. He pushed his shoulders off the wall, straightening to his full height, the better to see across the crowded room to the macao table. She was up to something. Every prickling hair on the nape of his neck told him so.

She was standing behind Charlie's chair, her fan moving in slow sweeps across the lower part of her face. She leaned forward to whisper something in Charlie's ear, and the rich swell of her breasts, the deep shadow of the cleft between them, was uninhibitedly revealed in the décolletage of her evening gown. Charlie looked up at her and smiled, the soft, infatuated smile of puppy love. It wasn't surprising this young cousin had fallen head over heels for Miss Judith Davenport, the marquis reflected. There was hardly a man in Brussels who wasn't stirred by her: a creature of opposites, vibrant, ebullient, sharply intelligent—a woman who in some indefinable fashion challenged a man, put him on his mettle one minute, and yet the next was as appealing as a kitten; a man wanted to pick her up and cuddle her, protect her from the storm . . .

Romantic nonsense! The marquis castigated himself severely for sounding like his cousin and half the young soldiers proudly sporting their regimentals in the salons of Brussels as the world waited for Napoleon to make his move. He'd been watching Judith Davenport weaving her spells for several weeks now, convinced she was an artful minx with a very clear agenda of her own. But for the life of him, he couldn't discover what it was.

His eyes rested on the young man sitting opposite Charlie. Sebastian Davenport held the bank. As beautiful as his sister in his own way, he sprawled in his chair, both clothing and posture radiating a studied carelessness. He was laughing across the table, lightly ruffling the cards in his hands. The mood at the table was lighthearted. It was a mood that always accompanied the Davenports. Presumably one reason why they were so popular . . . and then the marquis saw it.

It was the movement of her fan. There was a pattern to the slow sweeping motion. Sometimes the movement speeded, sometimes it paused, once or twice she snapped the fan closed, then almost immediately began a more vigorous wafting of the delicately painted half moon. There was renewed laughter at the table, and with a lazy sweep of his rake, Sebastian Davenport scooped toward him the pile of vowels and rouleaux in the center of the table.

The marquis walked across the room. As he reached the table, Charlie looked up with a rueful grin. "It's not my night, Marcus."

"It rarely is," Carrington said, taking snuff. "Be careful you don't find yourself in debt." Charlie heard the warning in the advice, for all that his cousin's voice was affably casual. A slight flush tinged the young man's cheekbones and he dropped his eyes to his cards again. Marcus was his guardian and tended to be unsympathetic when Charlie's gaming debts outran his quarterly allowance.

"Do you care to play, Lord Carrington?" Judith Davenport's soft voice spoke at the marquis's shoulder and he turned to look at her. She was smiling, her golden brown eyes luminous, framed in the thickest, curliest eyelashes he had ever seen. However, ten years spent avoiding the frequently blatant blandishments of maidens on the lookout for a rich husband had inured him to the cajolery of a pair of fine eyes.

"No. I suspect it wouldn't be my night either, Miss Davenport. *May* I escort you to the supper room? It must grow tedious, watching my cousin losing hand over fist." He offered a small bow and took her elbow without waiting for a response.

Judith stiffened, feeling the pressure of his hand cupping her bare arm. There was a hardness in his eyes that matched the firmness of his grip, and her scalp contracted as unease shivered across her skin. "On the contrary, my lord, I find the play most entertaining." She gave her arm a covert, experimental tug. His fingers gripped warmly and yet more firmly.

"But I insist, Miss Davenport. You will enjoy a glass of negus."

He had very black eyes and they carried a most unpleasant glitter, as insistent as his tone and words, both of which were drawing a degree of puzzled attention. Judith could see no discreet, graceful escape route. She laughed lightly. "You have convinced me, sir. But I prefer burnt champagne to negus."

"Easily arranged." He drew her arm through his and laid his free hand over hers, resting on his black silk sleeve. Judith felt manacled.

They walked through the card room in a silence that was as uncomfortable as it was pregnant. Had he guessed what was going on? Had he seen anything? How could she have given herself away? Or was it something Sebastian had done, said, looked . . . ? The questions and speculations raced through Judith's brain. She was barely acquainted with Marcus Devlin. He was too sophisticated, too hardheaded to be of use to herself and Sebastian, but she had the distinct sense that he would be an opponent to be reckoned with.

The supper room lay beyond the ballroom, but instead of guiding his companion around the waltzing couples and the ranks of seated chaperones against the wall, Marcus turned aside toward the long French windows opening onto a flagged terrace. A breeze stirred the heavy velvet curtains over an open door.

"I was under the impression we were going to have supper." Judith stopped abruptly.

"No, we're going to take a stroll in the night air," her escort informed her with a bland smile. "Do put one foot in front of the other, my dear ma'am, otherwise our progress might become a little uneven." An unmistakable jerk on her arm drew her forward with a stumble, and Judith rapidly adjusted her gait to match the leisured, purposeful stroll of her companion.

"I don't care for the night air," she hissed through her teeth, keeping a smile on her face. "It's very bad for the constitution and frequently results in the ague or rheumatism."

"Only for those in their dotage," he said, lifting thick black eyebrows. "I would have said you were not a day above twenty-two. Unless you're very skilled with powder and paint?"

He'd pinpointed her age exactly and the sense of being dismayingly out of her depth was intensified. "I'm not quite such an accomplished actress, my lord," she said coldly.

"Are you not?" He held the curtain aside for her and she found herself out on the terrace, lit by flambeaux set in sconces at intervals along the low parapet fronting the sweep of green lawn. "I would have sworn you were as accomplished as any on Drury Lane." The statement was accompanied by a penetrating stare.

Judith rallied her forces and responded to the comment as if it were a humorous compliment. "You're too kind, sir. I confess I've long envied the talent of Mrs. Siddons."

"Oh, you underestimate yourself," he said softly. They had reached the parapet and he stopped under the light of a torch. "You are playing some very pretty theatricals, Miss Davenport, you and your brother."

Judith drew herself up to her full height. It wasn't a

particularly impressive move when compared with her escort's breadth and stature, but it gave her an illusion of hauteur. "I don't know what you're talking about, my lord. It seems you've obliged me to accompany you in order to insult me with vague innuendoes."

"No, there's nothing vague about my accusations," he said. "However insulting they may be. I am assuming my cousin's card play will improve in your absence."

"What are you implying?" The color ebbed in her cheeks, then flooded back in a hot and revealing wave. Hastily she employed her fan in an effort to conceal her agitation.

The marquis caught her wrist and deftly twisted the fan from her hand. "You're most expert with a fan, madam."

"I beg your pardon?" She tried again for a lofty incomprehension, but with increasing lack of conviction.

"Don't continue this charade, Miss Davenport. It benefits neither of us. You and your brother may fleece as many fools as you can find as far as I'm concerned, but you'll leave my cousin alone."

Beneath a Sapphire Sea

by

Jessica Bryan

Rave reviews for Ms. Bryan's novels:

DAWN ON A JADE SEA

"Sensational! Fantastic! There are not enough superlatives to describe this romantic fantasy. A keeper!"
—*Rendezvous*

"An extraordinary tale of adventure, mystery and magic." —*Rave Reviews*

ACROSS A WINE-DARK SEA

"Thoroughly absorbing . . . A good read and a promising new author!" —*Nationally bestselling author Anne McCaffrey*

Beneath the shimmering, sunlit surface of the ocean there lives a race of rare and wondrous men and women. They have walked upon the land, but their true heritage is as beings of the sea. Now their people face a grave peril. And one woman holds the key to their survival. . . .

A scholar of sea lore, Meredith came to a Greek island to follow her academic pursuits. But when she encountered Galen, a proud, determined warrior of the sea, she was eternally linked with a world far more elusive and mysteriously seductive than her own. For she alone possessed a scroll that held the secrets of his people.

In the following scene, Meredith has just caught Galen searching for the mysterious scroll. His reaction catches them both by surprise . . .

He drew her closer, and Meredith did not resist. To look away from his face had become impossible. She felt something in him reach out for her, and something in her answered. It rose up in her like a tide, compelling beyond reason or thought. She lifted her arms and slowly put them around his broad shoulders. He tensed, as if she had startled him, then his whole body seemed to envelop hers as he pulled her against him and lowered his lips to hers.

His arms were like bands of steel, the thud of his heart deep and powerful as a drum, beating in a wild rhythm that echoed the same frantic cadence of Meredith's. His lips seared over hers. His breath was hot in her mouth, and the hard muscles of his bare upper thighs thrust against her lower belly, the bulge between them only lightly concealed by the thin material of his shorts.

Then, as quickly as their lips had come together, they parted.

Galen stared down into Meredith's face, his arms still locked around her slim, strong back. He was deeply shaken, far more than he cared to admit, even to himself. He had been totally focused on probing the landwoman's mind once and for all. Where had the driving urge to kiss her come from, descending on him with a need so strong it had overridden everything else?

He dropped his arms. "That was a mistake," he said, frowning. "I—"

"You're right." Whatever had taken hold of Meredith vanished like the "pop" of a soap bubble, leaving her feeling as though she had fallen headfirst into a cold sea. "It *was* a mistake," she said quickly. "Mine. Now if you'll just get out of here, we can both forget this unfortunate incident ever happened."

She stepped back from him, and Galen saw the anger in her eyes and, held deep below that anger, the hurt. It stung him. None of this was her fault. Whatever forces she exerted upon him, he was convinced she was completely unaware of them. He was equally certain she had no idea of the scroll's significance. To her it was simply an impressive artifact, a rare find that would no doubt gain her great recognition in this folklore profession of hers.

He could not allow that, of course. But the methods he had expected to succeed with her had not worked. He could try again—the very thought of pulling her back into her arms was a seductive one. It played on his senses with heady anticipation, shocking him at how easily this woman could distract him. He would have to find another less physical means of discovering where the scroll was.

"I did not mean it that way," he began in a gentle tone.

Meredith shook her head, refusing to be mollified. She was as taken aback as he by what had happened, and deeply chagrined as well. The fact that she had enjoyed the kiss—No, that was too calm a way of describing it. Galen's mouth had sent rivers of sensations coursing through her, sensations she had not known existed, and that just made the chagrin worse.

"I don't care what you meant," she said in a voice as stiff as her posture. "I've asked you to leave. I don't want to tell you again."

"Meredith, wait." He stepped forward, stopping just short of touching her. "I'm sorry about . . . Please believe my last wish is to offend you. But it does not change the fact that I still want to work with you. And whether you admit it or not, you need me."

"Need you?" Her tone grew frosty. "I don't see how."

"Then you don't see very much," he snapped. He paused to draw in a deep breath, then continued in a placating tone. "Who else can interpret the language on this sheet of paper for you?"

Meredith eyed him. If he was telling the truth, if he really could make sense out on those characters, then, despite the problems he presented, he was an answer to her prayers, to this obsession that would not let her go. She bent and picked up the fallen piece of paper.

"Prove it." She held it out to him. "What does this say?"

He ignored the paper, staring steadily at her. "We will work together, then?"

She frowned as she returned his stare, trying to probe whatever lay behind his handsome face. "Why is it so important to you that we do? I can see why you might think I need you, but what do you get out of this? What do you want, Galen?"

He took the paper from her. "*The season of destruction will soon be upon us and our city*," he read deliberately, "*but I may have found a way to save some of us, we who were once among the most powerful in the sea. Near the long and narrow island that is but a stone's throw from Crete, the island split by Mother Ocean into two halves . . .*"

He stopped. "It ends there." His voice was low and fierce, as fierce as his gaze, which seemed to reach out to grip her. "Are you satisfied now? Or do you require still more proof?"

TEMPTING EDEN
by
Maureen Reynolds

author of SMOKE EYES

"Ms. Reynolds blends steamy sensuality with
marvelous lovers. . . . delightful."
—*Romantic Times on SMOKE EYES*

Eden Victoria Lindsay knew it was foolish to break into the home of one of New York's most famous—and reclusive—private investigators. Now she had fifteen minutes to convince him that he shouldn't have her thrown in prison.

Shane O'Connor hardly knew what to make of the flaxen-haired aristocrat who'd scaled the wall of his Long Island mansion—except that she was in more danger than she suspected. In his line of work, trusting the wrong woman could get a man killed, but Shane is about to himself get taken in by this alluring and unconventional beauty. . . .

"She scaled the wall, sir," said Simon, Shane's stern butler.

Eden rolled her eyes. "Yes—yes, I did! And I'd do it again—a hundred times. How else could I reach the impossible *inaccessible* Mr. O'Connor?"

He watched her with a quiet intensity but it was Simon who answered, "If one wishes to speak with Mr. O'Connor, a meeting is usually arranged through the *proper* channels."

Honestly, Eden thought, the English aristocracy did not look down their noses half so well as these two!

O'Connor stepped gracefully out of the light and his

gaze, falling upon her, was like the steel of gunmetal. He leaned casually against the wall—his weight on one hip, his hands in his trousers pockets—and he studied her with half-veiled eyes.

"Have you informed the . . . ah . . . *lady*, Simon, what type of reception our unexpected guests might anticipate? Especially," he added in a deceptively soft tone, "those who scale the estate walls, and . . . er . . . shed their clothing?"

Eden stiffened, her face hot with color; he'd made it sound as if it were *commonplace* for women to scale his wall and undress.

Simon replied, "Ah, no, sir. In the melee, that particular formality slipped my mind."

"Do you suppose we should strip her first, or just torture her?"

"*What*?"

"Or would you rather we just arrest you, madame?"

"Sir, with your attitude it is a wonder you have a practice at all!"

"It is a wonder," he drawled coldly, "that you are still alive, madame. You're a damn fool to risk your neck as you did. Men have been shot merely for attempting it, and I'm amazed you weren't killed yourself."

Eden brightened. "Then I am to be commended, am I not? Congratulate me, sir, for accomplishing such a feat!"

Shane stared at her as if she were daft.

"And for my prowess you should be more than willing to give me your time. Please, just listen to my story! I promise I will pay you handsomely for your time!"

As her eyes met his, Eden began to feel hope seep from her. At her impassioned plea there was no softening in his chiseled features, or in his stony gaze. In a final attempt she gave him her most imploring look, and then instantly regretted it, for the light in his eyes suddenly burned brighter. It was as if he knew her game.

"State your business," O'Connor bit out.

"I need you to find my twin brother."

Shane frowned. "You have a twin?"

"Yes I do."

God help the world, he thought.

He leaned to crush out his cheroot, his gaze watching

her with a burning, probing intensity. "*Why* do you need me to find your twin?"

"Because he's missing, of course," she said in a mildly exasperated voice.

Shane brought his thumb and forefinger up to knead the bridge of his nose. "*Why*, do you need me to find him? *Why* do you think he is missing, and not on some drunken spree entertaining the . . . uh . . . 'ladies'?"

"Well, Mr. O'Connor, that's very astute of you—excuse me, do you have a headache, sir?"

"Not yet."

Eden hurried on. "Actually I might agree with you that Philip could be on a drunken spree, but the circumstances surrounding his disappearance don't match that observation."

Shane lifted a brow.

"You see, Philip *does* spend a good deal of time in the brothels, and there are three in particular that he frequents. But the madames of all of them told me they haven't seen him for several days."

Shane gave her a strange look. "You went into a brothel?"

"No. I went into *three*. And Philip wasn't in any of them." She thought she caught the tiniest flicker of amusement in his silver eyes, then quickly dismissed the notion. Unlikely the man had a drop of mirth in him.

"What do you mean by 'the circumstances matching the observation'?"

Eden suddenly realized she had not produced a shred of evidence. "Please turn around and look away from me Mr. O'Connor."

"Like hell."

Though her heart thudded hard, Eden smiled radiantly. "But you must! You have to!"

"I don't *have* to do anything I don't damn well please, madame."

"Please, Mr. O'Connor." Her tearing eyes betrayed her guise of confidence. "I-I brought some evidence I think might help you with the case—that is if you take it. But it's—I had to carry it under my skirt. Please," she begged softly.

Faintly amused, Shane shifted his gaze out toward the bay. Out of the corner of his eye he saw her twirl around, hoist her layers of petticoats to her waist, and fumble with something.

She turned around again, and with a dramatic flair that was completely artless, she opened the chamois bag she had tied to the waistband of her pantalets. She grabbed his hand and plopped a huge, uncut diamond into the center of his palm. Then she took hold of his other hand and plunked down another stone—an extraordinary grass-green emerald as large as the enormous diamond.

"Where," he asked in a hard drawl, "did you get these?"

"That," Eden said, "is what I've come to tell you."

OFFICIAL RULES

To enter the sweepstakes below carefully follow all instructions found elsewhere in this offer.

The **Winners Classic** will award prizes with the following approximate maximum values: 1 Grand Prize: $26,500 (or $25,000 cash alternate); 1 First Prize: $3,000; 5 Second Prizes: $400 each; 35 Third Prizes: $100 each; 1,000 Fourth Prizes: $7.50 each. Total maximum retail value of Winners Classic Sweepstakes is $42,500. Some presentations of this sweepstakes may contain individual entry numbers corresponding to one or more of the aforementioned prize levels. To determine the Winners, individual entry numbers will first be compared with the winning numbers preselected by computer. For winning numbers not returned, prizes will be awarded in random drawings from among all eligible entries received. Prize choices may be offered at various levels. If a winner chooses an automobile prize, all license and registration fees, taxes, destination charges and, other expenses not offered herein are the responsibility of the winner. If a winner chooses a trip, travel must be complete within one year from the time the prize is awarded. Minors must be accompanied by an adult. Travel companion(s) must also sign release of liability. Trips are subject to space and departure availability. Certain black-out dates may apply.

The following applies to the sweepstakes named above:

No purchase necessary. You can also enter the sweepstakes by sending your name and address to: P.O. Box 508, Gibbstown, N.J. 08027. Mail each entry separately. Sweepstakes begins 6/1/93. Entries must be received by 12/30/94. Not responsible for lost, late, damaged, misdirected, illegible or postage due mail. Mechanically reproduced entries are not eligible. All entries become property of the sponsor and will not be returned.

Prize Selection/Validations: Selection of winners will be conducted no later than 5:00 PM on January 28, 1995, by an independent judging organization whose decisions are final. Random drawings will be held at 1211 Avenue of the Americas, New York, N.Y. 10036. Entrants need not be present to win. Odds of winning are determined by total number of entries received. Circulation of this sweepstakes is estimated not to exceed 200 million. All prizes are guaranteed to be awarded and delivered to winners. Winners will be notified by mail and may be required to complete an affidavit of eligibility and release of liability which must be returned within 14 days of date on notification or alternate winners will be selected in a random drawing. Any prize notification letter or any prize returned to a participating sponsor, Bantam Doubleday Dell Publishing Group, Inc., its participating divisions or subsidiaries, or the independent judging organization as undeliverable will be awarded to an alternate winner. Prizes are not transferable. No substitution for prizes except as offered or as may be necessary due to unavailability, in which case a prize of equal or greater value will be awarded. Prizes will be awarded approximately 90 days after the drawing. All taxes are the sole responsibility of the winners. Entry constitutes permission (except where prohibited by law) to use winners' names, hometowns, and likenesses for publicity purposes without further or other compensation. Prizes won by minors will be awarded in the name of parent or legal guardian.

Participation: Sweepstakes open to residents of the United States and Canada, except for the province of Quebec. Sweepstakes sponsored by Bantam Doubleday Dell Publishing Group, Inc., (BDD), 1540 Broadway, New York, NY 10036. Versions of this sweepstakes with different graphics and prize choices will be offered in conjunction with various solicitations or promotions by different subsidiaries and divisions of BDD. Where applicable, winners will have their choice of any prize offered at level won. Employees of BDD, its divisions, subsidiaries, advertising agencies, independent judging organization, and their immediate family members are not eligible.

Canadian residents, in order to win, must first correctly answer a time limited arithmetical skill testing question. Void in Puerto Rico, Quebec and wherever prohibited or restricted by law. Subject to all federal, state, local and provincial laws and regulations. For a list of major prize winners (available after 1/29/95): send a self-addressed, stamped envelope entirely separate from your entry to: Sweepstakes Winners, P.O. Box 517, Gibbstown, NJ 08027. Requests must be received by 12/30/94. DO NOT SEND ANY OTHER CORRESPONDENCE TO THIS P.O. BOX.

SWP 7/93